CAPTAIN HOTNESS

WESTON PARKER

JEREMY

"So tell me about yourself." The busty blonde across the table from me leaned closer and smiled. Her ruby red lips would look damn good wrapped around my cock, but that was about as far as I figured things would go with us. Sex. Nothing more.

"I've already told you about myself, Sadie. Your turn." I forced a smile and tried like hell to hide my desire to get up and walk out.

The white table clothes and decorative chandeliers were too much. Couple that with a bunch of over-aged men shoving their potbelly's in suits and pretending to wait tables, and I was over it. I hated inauthentic people and places. And this place?

I glanced around and forced myself *not* to roll my eyes. It was a waste of my time, which was painful. Life seemed to be fucking flying by at break-neck speed.

Why my mother thought to set me up on a date at the most expensive restaurant in all of New Hampshire was beyond me. And to pair me up with a gold digger was almost funny. I didn't have the money my family had. I didn't want it.

"I'm nothing special." Sadie glanced down at the table. The subtle smirk on the side of her mouth gave away her false humility.

"No?" I leaned back and picked up the glass of wine in front of me. Why the fuck had I agreed to share a bottle of wine with her? Right. Get her drunk, naked in the back of my car on a dirt road and give her part of what she was after.

First my dick, and then my money, but the joke was on her. I didn't have a fat-ass bank account. I had a life I could be proud of. One where I worked hard and saved lives every day. The pretty girl whose foot was sliding up my leg didn't have a clue.

"Not really." She glanced up, and her blue eyes filled with a foreign emotion. Maybe she didn't want to be there either. What a novel thought.

"You like places like this?" I glanced around and noticed her pulling at her tits as I turned my attention from her. She was trying to seduce me. How cute. I'd have to give in a little just to make sure she didn't walk away completely empty-handed.

"I do." She reached down and picked up her phone as it buzzed. "I need to take this. I'll be right back."

"Sure." I pulled my phone out to play a game while I waited for her, but not before checking out her ass in her tight cream-colored skirt. She seemed the kind of woman who had been around the block a few million times. Where I wasn't interested in a virgin, I wasn't really turned on by the idea of sharing my bed with a whore either.

My phone buzzed as if on cue. My mother.

"Fuck." I hit the button to take the call and pulled the phone to my ear. "Hi, Mom."

"Jeremy. Why haven't you texted me? Are you still on the date with Sadie?"

"Yeah." I snorted. "Why would I call you? I'm a thirty-two-year-old man. I don't need to check in with you every ten minutes."

"Don't get snappy with me." Her tone turned to ice. "How is she? I think she's the one with the great idea on how to help solve the hunger issue here in New Hampshire. Her dad is our Governor."

"Not a chance, Mom. Check your notes. This girl looks like she swings around poles after hours." I pursed my lips at the sound of my mother losing her shit. Where I loved her like crazy, I hated how inte-grated she'd become in my life. My dating life in particular. I didn't need to find someone else. I was good. Laila was gone, and there was nothing I could do about it.

The very thought of standing over her grave stilled my heart. I missed her like a mother fucker, and I hadn't wanted to replace her.

"Jeremy. Are you still there?" My mom's tone softened a little.

"Yes. I'm on the date. I'll let you know how it goes tomorrow. She's not exactly my type-"

"Yes. She. Is." My mother huffed. "All of these women are great ladies and would be so good for Austin."

"Gotta go. I'll talk to you later." I dropped the call and put the phone back in my pocket. My five-year-old little boy didn't need a make-shift mom. He needed his mom back, but that wasn't going to happen.

"Hey. You okay?" Sadie sat down across from me with worry on her pretty face.

"Yeah. I'm just ready to get out of here." I tossed my napkin over the plate of half-eaten food in front of me. "I'm not feeling so good anymore. Let me give you a ride back home."

"Really?" Her bottom lip pushed out, and she was rather cute when she pouted. "I usually text my sister to get me out of most blind-date situations, but I was really excited about this one. I was hoping..." She stood and moved up beside me as we walked toward the door.

"For a night in my bed?" I glanced over at her and took her hand in mine as I walked up to the door. "I'm not sure that's a good idea. I'm in a weird place."

"Is it me?" She asked as we walked out into the chilly night's air. It hadn't started snowing just yet, but it was going to soon. I could almost smell it in the air.

"No. Hell no." I turned to face her and reached out to touch her cheek. "You're beautiful and smart. Why would it be you."

Not all lies. A stretch of the truth on the smarts, but she was fucking hot.

"Then take me home with you." She moved back as the valet pulled the car up.

I reached around and opened the door for her without replying. The valet gave me an eyebrow wag as I walked around to the other side. Man code for 'good luck with that hot piece of ass.'

"She's my sister, mother fucker." I gave him a stern look over the top of the car and rather enjoyed watching him stumble over his words as he paled. I got in the car without another word and buckled up.

"Jeremy. Please. Just for the night. I promise you won't regret it."

"Maybe on our next date." I pulled out and headed toward her place. Passing up a good long fuck was something I was going to regret later that night, but not the next morning. I didn't need another crazy bitch in my life. I had my sister and my mother. The thought of Nina made me smile. My older sister was all up in my shit too but in a good way. She was like a best friend that told it like it was. There was no placating her or trying to pull one over on her. She'd pin me to the floor mentally or physically. She was my hero. And maybe in some crazy way - I was hers.

"Well, how about a teaser of what could happen?" Sadie unbuckled and leaned over the console. She pressed her lips to the side of my neck and ran her hand between my thighs, waking my cock up. I groaned at the contact. I hadn't been with too many women since Laila's death, and all of them I had fucked had been quick and dirty. I couldn't even remember what the fuck it felt like to make love to someone.

My chest ached at the idea of it. I wasn't sure I'd ever be able to let my guard down and let someone in. And even if I could, would the woman accept the fact that I'd always be in love with my first wife? My high school sweetheart. My girl. My everything.

"God, you're big." Sadie brushed her nose up my neck and sucked on my ear.

Heat burned through my stomach as the blood rushed from my body to my dick. It swelled up nice and thick for her.

"Suck me off." I reached down and unzipped my jeans. "And no spitting. I don't allow that shit."

She smiled. "Absolutely."

I leaned the seat back a little and gripped the steering wheel as she worked my pants further open. A loud moan left me as she reached my cock. Her hands were cold, and my body was on fire. Pulling off on the side of the road, I stopped the car about the time she swirled her tongue around the thick head of my dick.

Her turn to moan.

Slipping my fingers into her hair, I gripped tightly and held her in place as I lifted my hips. Wet warmth surrounded me, and my balls tightened. I was going to unleash quite an orgasm on the poor girl seeing that I hadn't come for weeks.

My thighs shook as she took all eight inches, her skill beyond anything I'd seen in a long ass time. I reached over and gripped her skirt where it rested against the back of her thighs with my free hand. It took a few tugs to get the tight-ass thing up, but when I finally did, I wasted no time squeezing her pert ass and sliding my fingers under her panties to play with her holes.

"Fuck. Slow down, Sadie. I'm gonna come far too fast." I pulled at her hair, forcing her back up for a second as I pressed two fingers into her wetness and slipped my thumb into her ass. "You're good at that, girl."

"I love it." She reached down and stroked my sloppy wet dick while rolling her hips and fucking herself. The girl wasn't innocent in the slightest, and my first thoughts of her being with more men than I had on my team at the firehouse left me a little less interested in continuing our fuckfest.

"Good. Don't stop." I pulled her back down and pumped my hips a little, fucking her tight mouth until every cell in my body screamed for release. Her pussy and ass tugged at my fingers as she contracted in her own orgasm. Wetness filled the palm of my hand, and that's all I needed.

I moaned and released, filling her with my seed. It took everything inside of me not to call out Laila's name. Every woman was her and would forever be. It was the main reason I was fucked. I couldn't let go. No matter how hard I tried.

"You taste like heaven." She moved back, and I pulled my hand from her panties.

"Good. Glad you enjoyed it. You feel like heaven." I blurted out the first thing that came to me, though it wasn't true. Heaven was reserved for my wife's arms, her soft body, her big heart.

"So..."

I worked my cock back into my slacks and pulled back onto the road. Just a few more turns and she would be out of the car and out of my life. It was reckless to let anything happen between us, but I was needy. My record with women had me wanting to lock myself behind closed doors and become celibate.

As if.

"So what?" I pulled up to her place and stopped the car.

She glanced over at me with a bit of disenchantment on her pretty face. "So, we're not going back to your place?"

"No. I'm not interested in anything long term. I enjoyed dinner, and the blowjob on the side of the road was incredible, but I can't pretend or lead you on, Sadie. That's not fair." I unlocked the door. "Thanks again for a great evening."

"What? No. That's not acceptable. Your mother said you were looking for a wife."

"She lied." Anger swelled deep inside of me. "Get out. Please."

"Fine, but you're going to feel like shit in the morning when you think about the fact that you used me."

"Used you?" I gave her an incredulous look as she got out of the car and leaned back down to give me more shit. "I'm pretty sure you used me just as much."

"Whatever." She flipped me off and walked away from the car. "I hate you. I hate all men."

"But you like to suck dick. Odd." I drove away, having mumbled the last bit under my breath.

The loud smack to the back window had me chuckling. Another lost shoe on my account. It was the same with all of them.

Use their bodies to do whatever they could to draw me in.

But it was about more than that... it was so much deeper than a fuck. And no one had been willing to go there with me yet.

Not that I wanted anyone too anyway.

Laila was the only girl for me. Period.

2

BAILEY

"No. No. No." I dropped my paintbrush in the muddy colored water that floated around my favorite coffee mug. The picture before me was off. "More like it looks like shit. Why do I even try?"

I glanced at the clock next to my easel and let out a squeak. I was going to be late. Dammit.

Racing around the apartment, I got dressed in a button up white shirt and pair of black slacks. After pulling my long hair into a ponytail, I brushed my teeth and raced toward the door. My beat-up Toyota was going to have to behave, or I'd really be late to the restaurant.

I turned the music up in the car and tried to get my thoughts off my failing dreams and hopes. I'd never be an artist. I couldn't get the shading right or the contours perfect. I needed training, but good luck with that shit.

My family was all sorts of poor. Middle class was the proper term, but in was a wide net that caught too many people. My family was on the shallow end of the wealth pool, but it was fine. We didn't need money. We had each other.

I pulled up to the restaurant and tripped getting out of the car. The concrete below was less than pliable.

"Fuck." I got up and dusted my knees off as tears welled up in my eyes. "It would be so fantastic if just one damn thing would go right today."

"Just today?" Ellen, a friend from the restaurant and about the only girl I could tolerate at the Blackhouse Grille. "Be careful what you wish for. You just might get it."

I glanced down at my palms, which were torn up and bloody. "Every day. Let me update that wish to cover every day."

"It's going to get better." She shut the door to the car and rubbed my upper back as we walked toward the door at the back of the restaurant. "You're in a new place and don't know a soul. It's a weird place to be, but if it's any consolation at all, we're all pretty in awe of you."

"Why is that?" I opened the door and smiled. My brother said, 'why is that' all the fucking time like he couldn't think of anything else to say. He rubbed off on all of us who got a few minutes in the warmth of his personality. Especially me. A sadness I thought I'd gotten overran through the center of my chest. I missed Rhys, but it was time to grow up. I wasn't in the Air Force, and he was. I needed to start my own life off the base and stop taking up all of his time. I was his little sister, and if he ever planned to get married or date anyone for real, I needed to get out of his way.

So I moved. Far, far away. And regretted the shit out of it now that I was alone in a new city.

"I don't know." Ellen shrugged. "It just seems like a really big thing. You moved away from your family and the comfort of the things you knew to start over." She bumped her shoulder against mine. "You put yourself in this crazy-ass situation, and you're doing really good. Look at how well you've turned the restaurant around."

I nodded. I had done some good at the restaurant. Before over-hauling the menu and cleaning up the look of the place, I'd had a long, stern talk with every employee - one on one. It was a big job, but somehow I'd pulled it off. A spark of hope swelled in the pit of my stomach. Maybe Ellen was right. Maybe I was in the right place.

Now to find love. Someone who could hold me at night and spend my off days helping me figure out where I wanted to go with my artistic talents and such. That was a pipe dream I often tried to squash back down. It hurt too much to think it might never happen.

"Well, thanks. I appreciate that." I walked into the kitchen and nodded at a few of the chef's before making my way to my office. Ellen followed closely behind me.

"Okay, so how was the weekend? Did you go out like I suggested?"

I snorted. "No. I don't have anyone to go out with."

"Then we'll do something together this coming weekend."

"No." I sat down at my desk and pulled out a long list of things I had to get done before clocking back out. The owner had started to rely on me maybe a little *too* much. "I really don't have time for anything right now."

"Well, I'm making time." She turned and hopped up on my desk, crossing her legs and looking too cute for her own good. "Speaking of... can I get off just a little early tonight if things are slow around here?"

"Sure." I tried not to ask, but I couldn't help myself. "Why? You got something going on?" What I wouldn't have given for me to be the one with something going on. Hell, anything.

"I'm going to meet up with this new guy I met online." She shrugged and smiled so hard it had to have hurt her face.

"And you don't know anything about him?" I turned and gave her my full attention. "Cause not everything you see or read online is true."

"I know, but I'm willing to take a few risks." She glanced toward the door and back at me. "We're going to a really populated place. Like tons of people around."

"Why are you blushing?" I lifted an eyebrow and hated myself for asking. The deeper I dug, the more she would talk. I enjoyed her more than most people at the restaurant, but I wasn't looking for a girl-pal.

I liked my alone time. It gave me the chance to push myself a little more with my painting.

"Well." She glanced back at the door and then to me. "Don't say anything to anyone. You promise?"

"Who the fuck do I talk to?" I chuckled and leaned back in my chair, wishing I had something blush-worthy to share.

"Last night we sort of, um..." She glanced down at her hands. "We masturbated online."

"What?" I stiffened. The thought of masturbating in front of anyone was rather terrifying and yet, insanely hot. "Like with your computer camera on?"

She looked up and nodded. "It was so hot. It was hard to come, but I eventually got there."

I swallowed hard. I'd heard a few of Ellen's sexual exploits since coming to the restaurant, but nothing like this. "Was he... hot?"

"Oh yeah." She smiled. "And his dick was huge."

I shook my head. "Okay. TMI. Get out. I have shit to do. You need to be careful tonight. It's scary out there."

"Yeah." She got off the desk and laughed. "Be careful of baseball bat sized cocks."

"Out!" I turned to my paperwork and ignored how badly I was panting. "And close the door on your way you."

"Okay. Let me off early!" She laughed and closed the door behind her.

I leaned back in my chair and closed my eyes. I'd been in a few pathetic relationships over the last few years, but nothing like I read in my romance novels. I wanted a man to turn me on, to wake me up, to sweep me off my feet.

"No. To fuck me senseless." I grabbed a pen and tried to ignore the deep thumping desire that had my pussy contracting and my nipples tightening. Masturbating with someone online? Could I ever do that?

"Not a chance in hell." I took a shaky breath and worked on orders until the dinner rush hit. Then I was off my ass, running around the restaurant, helping in any and every way that I could. The evening slowed a little, and Ellen gave me a puppy dog expression.

"Can I go? Please?" She bounced on her feet and smiled.

I laughed. "Yeah. Just have a good time for both of us, hm?"

"You could come with us. You know I'm good with sharing." She wagged her eyebrows. "And let me tell you, there's plenty of inches to share."

"Oh God. Get out of here." I shooed her away and walked to the back of the restaurant. The other night manager, Tanner glanced up from the desk and smiled.

"Get out of here. You're on early shift."

"No. I'm good." I leaned against the frame of the door and studied him. His thin shoulders and lanky body didn't do anything for me, but I never could get the kind of guy that really turned me on. They didn't seem to notice me.

Guys like Jeremy Bennett. My brother, Rhys's best friend from high school. The guy was a God. Even back then. The last time I'd seen him was when I was still a kid, but he wasn't lanky or small at all. His baseball pants were always so tight, and I could make out the outline of his dick perfectly. Every part of me was turned on by him, even now. Years later and I still wished I were old enough to make him take notice of me back then.

"Hey. I'm serious. Get out of here, beautiful. Enjoy your night." Tanner smiled.

He was sweet and kind, but that's about all.

"Okay. Yeah. Thanks." I grabbed my keys and walked out the back door. The icy cold air of autumn whipped around me. It would be winter soon, and though I knew how to drive in the snow, I hated it all the same.

The ride home was dull and lonely. I kept thinking about how much fun Ellen had to be having. She'd have dinner and drinks with Mr. Monster Cock and then end up pressed against a wall, getting her wildest fantasies taken care of. I imagined all of mine as I made my way back to the apartment.

By the time I got there, my body was on fire. It had been forever since I let myself even think about lusty things. It never worked really well for me. I'd want and want and want, and that's where it stopped. It never moved into having, getting, fulfilling.

"Fuck this life." I walked into my apartment and closed the door behind me. After dropping my purse and kicking off my shoes, I walked to the kitchen and leaned over, pressing my forearms to the counter. I wanted someone to greet me when I walked in, and not a normal greeting. An aggressive, get on your knees and suck every inch of this monster cock greeting. He'd work himself deep into my throat before taking me right there on the floor.

In my mouth. My pussy. My ass.

A groan left me that chilled my desire. It wasn't going to happen. It hadn't yet, and there was no hope in sight. And the saddest part was as much as I wanted love, I yearned for lust so much more.

3

JEREMY

"Fuck this day." Mayhem walked in and dropped down in front of my desk after a long ass Monday at the fire station.

"Oh yeah?" I glanced up from a pile of papers I had to deal with. "Is the second crew still out at the Beckham place?"

"Yes. They almost have it taken care of, but they need to hurry the fuck back."

"Why is that?" I leaned back and lifted my hands, cupping them behind my head. "You dating one of the guys in the group?"

"Up yours, Cap." He shook his head and gave me a stern look. "We're a man short on my crew because Davis' wife is having another damn kid. I swear that idiot doesn't know how to keep his cock in his pants. He needs to get a few more channels on his TV."

I snorted. "Because watching TV would help him keep his hands off his wife? Have you seen Silvia?"

"Yeah. She's fine as shit, but come on. Five kids, Jeremy. That's insane."

"I like the idea of a big family." I glanced over at the picture I had of Laila and Austin when the little guy was just two. "It's not in the cards for me anymore, but it's something I would have wanted."

"No talking about Laila." Mayhem stood and lifted his arms toward the ceiling. "So how are things going?"

"What things are you referring to?" I leaned back farther in my chair and lifted my legs to drop my feet on the desk.

"Your dating life. Tell me about the latest shit your mother got you involved in. Nothing makes my day better than hearing your stories."

"That so?" I lifted my eyebrow and stifled a laugh. "You like the fact that my mother is trying to find me a wife like the old days?"

"I fucking love it." He ran his hands over his head and laughed loudly. "My mom gave up on me a long time ago."

"You're a slut-puppy. We all gave up on you a long time ago." I glanced down to see who was calling my cell. Rhys. My best friend from high school, and one of Laila's favorite people on the planet. "I gotta take this. If you have a call to go out, just grab me. I'll take up Davis' spot. I'm a better firefighter than all of you pussy's put together."

"Pussy's put together? Like a pussy-wall?" His eyes grew wide, and a playful look moved across his face. "Can you imagine?"

"It's better than a dick-wall. Get outta here." I picked up the phone and pressed it to my ear. "Rhys. How are you, man?"

"Jeremy Bennett." Rhys laughed, and the sound of it warmed me. It was almost like I could imagine Laila being just behind me. "How is life treating you, brother?"

"It's good." I lied.

"Bull shit." He chuckled.

I stood and walked toward the lone window in my office. "It's life man. Nothing has been right for the last few years, but you know that."

"Yeah. I miss our girl every day, brother."

"Me too." I ran my hand down my face and tried like hell not to crack. I'd spent too many nights on the floor in the bedroom or the bathroom crying my guts out over what I'd lost. At times it almost seemed like never loving her would have been easier, but I didn't have the option. She'd swept into mine and Rhys's life like a whirlwind. The love triangle lasted all of a week and then she was my girlfriend and Rhys's bestie. It worked until it didn't.

"On a better note, what're your plans for the holidays? I'm finally headed up your way."

"Are you?" I pulled myself from the pit of despair I was headed toward full speed ahead. "What's bringing you up here, man? You tired of the flatlands in Illinois?"

"Naw. I love this place. My job gives me all I need."

"Oh, it fucks you from time to time too?" I laughed as he snorted.

"No. I have some honey's here on base for that shit. You know how women feel about a man in uniform."

"I see you're still a complete scoundrel."

"I do try." He cleared his throat. "I'm headed up there because Bailey moved up that way about six months ago."

"Your baby sister?" I walked back to my chair and sat down as a smile spread across my lips. That poor girl had been nothing but legs and pigtails. She was one of the guys as often as Rhys would let her be. I hadn't seen her in ten years or more, and she was sixteen. Cute, but nothing I'd give a second glance to.

"That's the one. She's not a baby anymore."

"I bet not." I dropped down in my chair. "Where is she? I've probably bumped into her if it's over here by the fire station."

"She's not too far from you guys. I just mapped it today. You wouldn't recognize her, Jer. She's not a little girl anymore. Stupid ass."

I smiled. "I'm sure not. Remember she had a huge crush on me when we were kids."

"Don't go there. She's six years younger than you, Cougar."

"Naw... I'm not going there. I'm glad to hear you're coming up this way. Tell me where she is so I can stop by and let her know I'm the Fire Chief over here. If she needs anyone, I'm happy to help her man. You're like family to me."

"Same. I think she would like that." He gave a pregnant pause, and I jumped in to reassure him.

"I'm not going to try anything, Rhys. I'm still lost to Laila. I'm not sure I'll ever be with anyone else, man. Seriously. And if we're being honest, Bailey probably isn't my type. I like sweet girls."

He laughed. "Fucking liar. She's exactly your type, but I do trust you. She's running Blackhouse Grille about a mile from you."

"I love that place." I glanced up as the sirens went ape-shit. "Gotta run. I'll check in with her soon. Maybe she needs a trusted friend if nothing else."

"I like the sound of that. I'll be in touch brother. Be safe."

"Same to you." I dropped the call and ran out into the hallway to get dressed and get my ass on the firetruck. Mayhem was in charge, and though I could have easily taken the reigns from him, I played second and moved where he told me to be, just allowing myself to be one of the guys for the call.

"What are we looking at?" I asked Mayhem.

"It's a building fire. It's out of control, but all of the residents are safely out of there. It's a younger crowd, so they hauled ass out of the building when they smelled smoke. We just need to get the damn thing under control before it moves to the building next to it, which isn't such a young crowd."

"We need to get someone busy getting everyone out of the building on either side of it." I pulled out my phone and made a few quick calls as energy raced through me. I'd taken the captain spot a few years back because Laila wanted me off the front line. I understood the concern and respected her wishes. I was the youngest captain in the northeast, but it was a spot I earned with ten years of hard work and lots of fucking 'yes Sirs.'

We pulled up to the blaze and the crew hustled off the truck, going into action. The heat from the fire was blistering. I'd almost forgotten how incredibly hot the inferno could get. Sweat dripped down my back and over my chest as I moved into place and worked beside my men.

It was hard as fuck not taking back over from Mayhem, but I managed to keep my lips sealed for most of the evening.

"We're losing pressure," Nam yelled from in front of me.

"Fuck." I moved out of place and forced the guys to shuffle up to keep fighting with the tools we had. Pulling off my helmet, I jogged back to the street where the hose was locked into a fire hydrant. Kneeling, I tightened it and cursed the guys. Someone hadn't done their job correctly with the hose, which cost time and put all of us in danger.

The thought of Austin losing another parent had me moving twice as fast as I wanted too. My little boy didn't need another tragedy in his life. He'd barely survived the first one.

"Got it?" Mayhem yelled over the roar of the fire.

"Yes. Let's finish this and regroup." I moved back into place and helped the guys to put the fire out.

We gathered our equipment and ignored the media and crowds as we moved back to the truck. I stepped up and took a turn looking at each of the guys.

"Hey. You've all been trained to do your job and do it well and fast." I turned to Mayhem. "The hose was too loose on the goddamn hydrant. We're going to spend all day tomorrow retraining on that." I glanced back at the guys. "You mess up in a small way, and you could fuck us all. Got it? There are no second chances when you're at the front lines of a fire."

"Yes, Sir." They all took turns responding to me.

"I'm sorry, Captain. We'll retrain again tomorrow." Mayhem patted me on the back as we walked back to the truck. I was proud of him for not throwing the rookie that hooked the hose up wrong under the bus. It was the signs of a good leader and a good man.

A man I was proud to have on my team.

We rode back with the guys singing their guts out to a Taylor Swift song. I was first off the truck. Weariness pulled at me. I needed to find a way to get more sleep. I was in great shape physically thanks to hours in the gym and working out with the crew, but emotionally and mentally, I was struggling. Laila's birthday was just around the corner, and I could feel it closing in like icy fingers on my soul.

I took a quick shower, texted Nina that I was headed to the house and drove home in silence. My conversation with Rhys filled my thoughts. It was going to be good to see Bailey after all the years that had passed. I was curious what she looked like and how she'd turned out.

A smile touched my lips as I parked my truck beside my bike, Nina's Mercedes and the Mustang I just *had* to have. My midlife crises came early.

The lights were on the small two-bedroom house I had, and I could see my sister and Austin running around the living room together.

I opened the door and closed it loudly. "Who's making all that noise in here?"

"Daddy!" Austin's little voice warmed me to the depths of my soul. He had my energy and Laila's features. I loved him beyond belief, but him looking like his momma made me want to love him more, deeper, stronger.

"Hey, buddy!" I bent down and picked him up.

He snuggled against me and let out a long sigh. "You smell like BBQ."

"Yeah? That's kinda gross." I kissed his head and walked into the living room.

Nina glanced up from the floor and smiled. "I hope I have ten kids with as much energy as Austin."

"Why is that?" I sat down on the couch and watched her. How a strong, beautiful woman like her hadn't settled down was beyond me. Yet another mystery in my weird, fucked up life.

"Because, little brother, payback is hell." She stood, walked over and kissed the top of my head before leaning down and tickling Austin.

"No, Aunt Nina! No!" He wiggled in my arms, and I turned as best as I could, pretending to shelter him from Nina's attack.

"Get outta here with that." I let Austin go and stood up. "You staying the night?"

"Hell no. You're a useless human being when you have someone around." She picked up her purse and walked to the door.

"Go to your room for a few minutes and clean up Champ." I patted

Austin on the head and followed my sister to the back door. "I'm going to see Aunt Nina out."

"Clean up? Ugh." Austin's little voice caused me to chuckle.

"Life is so hard when you're five, right?" I opened the door for my sister.

"I think it's hard at every stage, but that's just me." She walked out and bounded down the stairs before turning back to face me. "How was the date?"

"Horrible. Don't ask."

She gave me a look. "You need to tell Mom to back off."

"No, you need to tell her. She doesn't listen to me."

"Accept the billions of dollars she has in the bank with your name on it, and she'll probably leave you alone." She dove into the same speech she always did. "Daddy left that money to you, Jer."

"I know. I don't want to do this tonight. I love you very much. The date sucked, literally."

"Eww... Too much info." She turned and walked toward the car. "I love you too."

I closed the door and walked into Austin's room. He was in his bed, reading a book, or trying to.

"Need some help?" I pulled off my boots and walked toward his little bed before crawling in next to him.

"Nope. I'll read it to you."

"Please do." I let out a long yawn and pulled him against me. His little voice droned on as he tried to read whatever book he had in his hands. I only heard a few minutes of it before darkness swept in and took me to the only place my sweet girl still lived.

My dreams.

4

BAILEY

"Well. Good for you." Ellen sounded rather approving as I held the phone to my ear. I stood just outside the Currier Museum of Art. It was my day off hangout place. Every time I had a day off.

The greeter at the door smiled as he turned my way. "Morning, Miss Wright! Oh, sorry. Didn't see the phone."

"No problem." I nodded and moved away from the building. There was no way in hell I was going into the quiet, majestic halls with Ellen talking to me about her eight-inch cock conquest. It just felt - wrong. I turned my attention back to the call. "Yeah. I need a new place to go on my days off, but this one is still doing it for me."

"You need a man. Period." She sounded as if she were spot on where my problems laid.

"Yeah. Right." I glanced around and took in the beautiful serenity around me. "Like I need a hole in the head."

"Bailey. Jared was exactly the kind of guy you should be with."

"Mr. Eight inches?" I laughed and turned away from the poor guy that walked in front of me about the time I mumbled my nasty response. "No thank you. I haven't been with anyone in a really long time."

"Define a long time." She seemed to hold her breath as there was *no* sound coming from the phone.

"Like... ever." I shrugged and glanced back at the museum.

"You're a virgin! What the hell? Have you ever seen a dick?"

"Yes, I've seen one. I've given a few blowjobs and-" I turned the other way as a grandmother walked past me quickly with three kids. I was going to hell. "I'm not having this conversation here. We can talk about this over wine."

"How are you a virgin?" she yelled much louder than necessary.

"Because I haven't found the right guy. Shit." I turned and faced the museum as my stomach tightened. I couldn't sleep around. I just couldn't do it. I wanted lust so fucking bad, and yet when it got right down to doing the dirty deed... I couldn't do it. I couldn't push past the idea that I was giving the guy above me, behind me, below me something that he wouldn't cherish. It was my innocence. It was just about all I had left to offer anyone.

"The right guy? Well, from someone who has slept around her *whole life* and I do mean *whole life*, sex is amazing. It's not something you want to miss out on. People pay for it for goodness sakes. It's like a delicious high. A drug."

"Hey. Doctor Ruth. Slow your roll. I'm not talking about this over the phone. I'm hanging up now. It's museum day, okay?"

"This conversation isn't over-"

I dropped the call, put the phone on silent and walked back toward the door. The greeter, Thomas gave me a nod.

"Everything okay, today?" His smile was warm and reminded me of my grandfather on my mother's side.

"Yeah. Just a friend who has no relationship trying to give out relationship counseling." I smiled.

He chuckled and opened the door wider. "Well, a beautiful woman like you doesn't need advice, she needs high standards, which I'm sure you have, Miss Wright."

"That I do." I walked in and waved before mumbling under my breath. "And it's probably half the reason I'm still alone."

Stopping just inside the door, I breathed in deeply and let the beauty before me settle my soul. I'd never be anything too special, nor would I probably figure out how to sell my art or even create a piece that I'd consider letting someone see, but I could pretend. It was easy to do in the middle of the art museum where dreams seemed to come alive.

I moved up to a beautiful modern piece that used multiple mediums. The colors were rich and bold, and the aluminum and tin were twisted and manipulated to almost cause a 3D effect on the painting.

"I love it." I moved closer and tilted my head a little.

"I do too." A deep masculine voice resounded next to me. It was smooth. Sexy. Strong.

"Oh. Sorry." I moved to my right a little and tugged at the white cardigan I had over my blue blouse. My skirt was a mixture of both, and I regretted wearing sandals the minute I stepped out of the house seeing that my toes were turning purple and freezing.

"Nothing to be sorry about." He glanced down at me and smiled. His glasses looked good on him, as did the grey and white streaks in his black hair. His face was clean shaven, and his nose and cheekbones aristocratic. He was much too thin, but still a very good looking older man.

I turned back to the painting and tried to figure out my best plan of attack. I needed to move to something else, but I didn't want to appear rude. A million thoughts raced through my mind as I stood there, most of them around the conversation with Ellen. Why was she dating and having great sex and I was still stuck in my hopes for Mister Right? It seemed stupid and childish.

"The artist is from Columbia." He spoke again, and the beautiful way he said Columbia had me turning back to him. "It's multi-media art, and yet it has a hint of what Van Gogh was after, no?" He kept his eyes on the painting, but it felt like he was staring straight at me. There was something very powerful about him.

"I agree." I forced myself to turn back to it. "It reminds me a little of The Starry Night, but the colors are more in line with the upcoming holidays. Warm and rich." I took a shaky breath. I'd never really spoken to anyone about art before, and though it was silly, there was something almost sensual about it.

"Edward." He extended a card toward me. He held it between his first finger and middle finger, both longer than other guys I'd been around. His nails were perfectly manicured. I couldn't help but wonder if he minded getting his fingers dirty. Heat burned in the center of my stomach, and I felt flustered. What was wrong with me?

Was there an age a woman hit to where everything was about sex? The desire to be touched was almost overwhelming. It was silly. Stupid.

"What's this?" I took the card and tried hard to act about ten years older than I was.

"My card. I'd like to take you out for lunch? Dinner? Drinks?" He turned to face me. His dark blue eyes moved around my face but never went any lower. I was a little disappointed, but then again, I was turning into a member of the whore-core in my head.

"I'm Bailey."

"What you are is beautiful." He smiled softly. "Not in the way I'd usually be interested in, but you carry yourself as if you're protecting precious cargo."

I reached up and rubbed just above my left breast. "Heartbreak is no fun, and there are only so many times you can crumble before you don't want to get back up again."

"Poetic, Miss..."

"Wright. Baily Wright."

"Well, Miss Wright. You've captivated me today. Not an easy feat in the slightest." He nodded toward the card. "Call me. Let's get together and talk about the things that make both of us come alive."

"Like art?" I glanced down at the card feeling very immature and not nearly *enough* for the well-dressed, older man in front of me.

"Among other things." He took a step back. "Until then?"

"Enjoy your day." I turned back to the painting and waited for an excitement to race through me. Nothing. He wasn't my type, and where it was flattering that someone so good looking and well put together would stop to even talk to me, much less ask me out, it did nothing for me.

"Boo!" Ellen's voice sounded beside me.

"Shit!" I yelped and covered my mouth with my hand before giving an apologetic look to everyone standing around us. "Sorry."

"Hey. I wanted to surprise you." She wrapped an arm around my shoulders and squeezed. "You sounded so ugh a few minutes ago."

"What?" I whispered as softly as I could. "I was just being me."

"Well, let's be me and you together. I'm off today too, you know."

"I know." I moved out from under her arm and walked to the next painting. "You don't even like art."

"No, but you do, and I want to hang out. I need to recover from being drowned in hormones. Art galleries take it out of me like," she glanced around and gave me a look of boredom, "immediately."

I laughed softly. "I love this place."

"Right, but you're not getting laid." She lifted her eyebrow as if challenging me.

"Life isn't about sex." I held up the card. "And before you give me a nine inches lecture-"

"Eight inches." She held up her hands to show me a visual on the eight inches.

I pulled her hands down. "Right. Before you give me a lecture, I got asked out."

She snatched the card. "What? Who?" She glanced up and looked around before reading the card again. "Edward Neobalm? What kind of last name is that?"

"It's an older rich guy."

"How old?" She pulled the card just out of my reach. "We talking forties and hot or eighties and could be your grandfather."

"Probably late forties." I popped her in the stomach and took the card. "I'm not going to call him. He wasn't my type."

"He's twenty years older than you. Wonder why he's not your type." She gave me a look. "Wait. What is your type?"

I shrugged and stopped at a painting of two lovers, their bodies wrapped around each other. It was hard to tell where one began and the other ended. It caused a need to awaken in me again. I wanted so much more than I had.

"I'd say six foot four, two hundred pounds of muscle, handsome face, warm brown eyes, and brown hair." I wanted to reach out and touch the picture, but I forced myself not to. "He would be a baseball player or maybe an Air Force Pilot or even a fireman."

She laughed and forced me to turn toward her. "What's his name, Bailey?"

"Who?" I came up out of imaging what Jeremy looked like after all these years. "What's whose name?"

"The man you're describing." She lifted her eyebrow. "Tell me. Seriously."

"No clue what you're talking about, Ellen." I walked toward the side exit. "Come on. Let's grab a coffee. I'm tired of being here."

"You? Tired of the art museum?"

I nodded and walked back out into the chilly morning. I refused to tell her or anyone else how fragile my love of art was. One minute it had me soaring to the highest peaks because of its beauty and the promise that I'd find all the emotions it spoke of. And the next? I'd come to and realize that nothing in my life could be described as anything but a valley.

A long, lonely valley that I had to trek through alone.

5

JEREMY

"Look. Just get through it, and I promise you, we'll sit down and talk to momma together soon, okay?" My sister's voice should have been calming, but it wasn't.

My mother had decided to set me up on another fucking blind date and didn't tell me until the poor girl was already sitting at the table in the middle of the restaurant. The only reason I decided to go, besides the fact that I wasn't a total dick, was that it was at the Blackhouse Grille. The thought of walking in and reconnecting with little Bailey Wright had my mood not diving deep into the dumpster.

"This is fucked up. You're single for God's sakes. Why the hell isn't she setting you up? You're older! If we were in a foreign country, you'd be deemed damaged goods right now!" I barked playfully into the phone.

"Watch it, cockhead. Go in there and tell the girl that you're happy to be there. Tell her that your genital herpes have flared up, and you just didn't think you were going to make it." Nina barely made it through her last few words due to her incessant laughter.

"Ha. Ha. Fuck you too." I leaned back in my seat and breathed in deeply through my nose as the phone beeped in my ear. "Someone is trying to call."

"Well, it's the girl or momma. Check." She laughed harder.

"I hate you sometimes." I pulled the phone from my ear to see it was my mother. "It's Mom."

"Be nice. You know all she has is us."

"She's about to just have you and your damaged goods ass." I smiled. "I'll call you later. Thanks for keeping Austin on short notice."

"No worries, but we're going to my house. He likes the pool, and your place is booooring."

"Thanks." I flipped the call over, closed my eyes and answered. "Hey, Mom."

"Jeremy. Are you at the restaurant? Bethel called and said that Tazzy hadn't seen you yet."

"I was running late from work, Mother. You know a little bit of notice would be good. You literally informed me that I would be having dinner with Tazzy (I shuddered at the poor girl's name) about thirty minutes ago. I fight fires for a living."

"You're the captain. Don't try and pull anything over on me. I'm your mother."

"I'm going into the restaurant now. I'm going to come see you soon. I want this to end."

"What? Me trying to help you find a mother for my *only* grandson? It's been two years, Jeremy. It's time to move on. It's not fair to Austin or you. It's not fair to any of us."

"I'm sorry my wife dying isn't fair to anyone." Anger burned through me, crippling my resolve to get out of the car and tell *Tazzy* about my herpes or lack thereof. I'd have loved to pull it off just to get a good laugh out of Nina later.

"Jeremy Mitchell Bennett. Don't you dare throw this back on me or on Laila. Don't."

I swallowed and reached for the door. "I'm going into the restaurant. This is the last time I'm doing this for a while. Got it?"

"Fine. If you don't want my help, then you'll not get it."

"Good night, Mom." I dropped the call, put the fucking phone on silent and walked toward the old Grille. The place was a piece of shit, and one I rarely visited, but it looked better. Cleaner.

After locking the truck, I walked in and stopped short. "Shit."

The place looked brand new. Like someone had come in and cleaned it up from floor to ceiling. It was nice. Beyond nice.

"Hi, Sir. Table for one?" A young guy at the hostess stand gave me a warm smile.

"No. Meeting someone named Tazzy." I stared at him instead of looking around.

"Do you want to mosey around and see if you see her?"

"Nope. Blind date thanks to my meddling mother." I turned my attention up toward the bar. The girl working the counter had her back to me, but the long brown braid that touched the top of her ass caught my attention. I loved a woman who kept her hair up for the world and let it down for me. Laila always had short hair, but I begged her into long hair a few times much to my pleasure and her pain.

The girl had narrow shoulders and a tiny waist, but the swell of her hips was fucking hot.

"I'll find the girl. Thanks." I waved the young guy off and walked toward the bar. I wanted a good look at the bartender. No fucking way she was Bailey, but I could have a few well-hidden fantasies. My eyes moved down to the swell of the girl's ass in her tight black slacks, and I stifled a groan. Those hips and thighs, a big ass and long hair. Fuck me. She started to turn toward the bar, and I cut off to the left. No need to get myself into trouble with some random woman I wanted to see naked and nothing more.

My cock grew thick and hard in my jeans, which was fucked up. I made a beeline to the bathroom and walked in as someone called out my name. Tazzy most likely. I ignored her and closed the door behind me in the stall.

"Chill the fuck out." Pressing my hand to the front of my jeans, I wrapped my fingers around my erection and tried to catch my breath. It was a good-looking woman from behind. No biggie. She probably looked like a man from the front. Yeah. A lumberjack with a beard and shit. For sure. Hairy armpits and a bushy mound and...

"There." I breathed in deeply as my arousal faded into oblivion. The last thing I wanted to do was to admit to myself that I was a little turned on at the thought of the girl being Rhys's little sister all grown up. She had no clue, but I remembered the way she looked at me when I'd gone home from college with Rhys for his folk's fortieth wedding anniversary. I was twenty-two and she was sixteen. No fucking way I'd get near her, but I could almost sense the desire rolling off her.

Hormones. It had been puberty for sure. Girls didn't hit puberty until sixteen or seventeen. Right?

I ran my fingers through my hair and forced myself into a calmer demeanor. Just because Rhys's little sister was somewhere in the restaurant and she had the hots for me years ago didn't mean shit.

I was damaged goods. Not my sister like she often teased about. I was torn and broken and fucked up beyond repair. Hell, I didn't want to be repaired.

"Let it go. Idiot." I splashed water on my face and patted myself dry with a paper towel. I studied myself in the mirror and growled. I was getting older, and uglier. The hard days and nights of fighting fires were wearing on me. I had laugh lines and forehead lines and lines on the side of my eyes. "Stupid."

I was caught by surprise as I walked out of the bathroom and almost ran over a small, frail looking girl with wild red hair and big blue eyes.

"Jeremy?" She smiled, and rows of braces smiled back at me.

No, the fuck my mother didn't set me up with a high school junior.

"Um. Tazzy?" I forced a smile.

"Wow. You are so good looking. I knew you were a firefighter and stuff, but dayum." She lifted her hands in the air and danced a little like an old-time rapper. This shit wasn't happening. Surely I was going to wake up any fucking minute in a pool of my sweat.

"Thanks." I glanced around as my pulse spiked. This young pre-pubescent girl was supposed to be my date? Holy shit.

"Hey. I'm twenty-eight. I just never developed really well." She smiled and snorted.

My eyes widened. "Hey look. I hate to do this, but I just went into the bathroom and checked my shit, and my herpes are all flared up. It's really ugly down there. And the shit itches."

She gave me an odd look and glanced down to my dick and back up to me. "Wow. You sure? Do you need some cream or something?"

"I need a rain check." I shrugged and tried to look much nicer than I was. "That okay? Tazzy-girl?"

"Oh yeah. Sure." She gave me a sweet smile. "Let's do this weekend if you're feeling better. Maybe we can have dinner at my place." Another cheesy ass smile. "I can rub some cream on you if you need me to."

"Sounds like heaven." I winked, turned and walked into the bathroom in horror. My sister was going to have a fucking field day with that one. "You've got to be kidding me. How do I keep getting pulled into these ridiculous situations?"

I gave myself a few more minutes to make sure Tazzy was good and gone before going out. She was nowhere in sight as I walked out of the bathroom and let out a sigh of relief.

"Herpes? Really?" The pretty girl from the bar walked by, her voice soft and sexy.

"Hey. I had to make it about me. Come on." I turned and followed her. My eyes moved down to that fine ass again, and I could almost picture myself on my knees, my face pressed to it, my tongue fucking her as deep and as fast as she'd let me. "She would have thought it was about her."

"She knows it's about her." The girl turned the corner and walked into the back of the bar before turning to face me.

Her dark hair was pulled back in the sexy-ass braid, but little pieces of it flew out from around her beautiful face. It took me a minute to remember how to fucking talk. Her nose was cute as a button, her lips soft looking and a muted pink. The wisdom and playfulness in her light green eyes left my dick swelling again. Little freckles danced across her nose, and her cheeks were pink like her lips.

"God damn, woman." I pressed my hands to the bar and leaned in a little, still miles away from where I wanted to be. Her tits were perky and big enough to fill up my hands, which was all I needed. She had me wishing for far more than I should have been wishing for. It had been forever since I'd felt anything that powerful, that intoxicating. "You are so incredibly fine. Please tell me you're married."

"Try it on someone else, Jeremy. It's not happening here, buddy." She smiled, and realization washed over me. "No ring. I'm not interested."

"Bailey?" I dropped down in the seat next to me as my cock poked me in the stomach. I shifted uncomfortably and tried to keep my attention on her face. She wasn't a little girl anymore, and fuck me if she wasn't the best looking woman in all of New Hampshire. "Rhys told me you'd come up this way."

"Yeah?" She reached for a rag and wiped down the bar. "I wanted to start a new life, you know... one where my family wasn't at the very center of it."

"You have a great family." I wanted to get up and hug her, to pull her against me for so many reasons. Just seeing her and knowing who she was softened me. Rhys was my best friend, and outside of my little boy, he was all I had left to remember Laila by. The memories the three of us had together got me through some of the toughest shit imaginable, and yet, Bailey felt the same to me. Like having my wife and my best friend right in front of me.

"Hey. You okay?" Her voice softened as she walked around the counter to stand next to me.

My knuckles were white as I gripped the bar, and my breathing was all over the fucking place. I nodded. "Yeah. Sorry. Just so many memories of your brother and my wife."

"I'm so sorry for your loss, Jer." She reached out and squeezed my shoulder tightly. "I heard you have a little guy."

"I do." I pulled myself together fast and stood. "My mother keeps setting me up on these fucking dates."

She laughed, and the room brightened a little. "I don't have that problem. Just an overprotective brother that wouldn't let me date even if I wanted to."

"So no boyfriend, hm?" I slipped my hands into my pockets and studied her. I wanted to see that same desire she'd had as a girl when she looked at me, but it wasn't there. Not that I could tell.

"No." She smiled and walked back around the bar. "Well, I gotta get back to work, and from what I can tell," She paused and looked around, "the coast is clear for you."

I laughed and stood there for a second more. "It's good to see you, Bailey. You look real good. All grown up."

"That happens when you blink a few times." She winked at me and turned her back to me. "See you around."

"Yeah. You will." I turned and walked to the front door of the restaurant. What a strange turn of events.

It wasn't her that had lust in her eyes when she looked at me.

It was me this time, looking at her.

6

BAILEY

"So beautiful, Bailey." *Jeremy's voice was commanding but loving.*

I glanced over my shoulder as I rode him reverse cowgirl. In my dreams, I didn't have to worry what the fuck to do. It all worked out somehow.

"You like that?" I gripped his thick thighs and slid down his shaft, taking him back inside of me. Pleasure pulsed in my stomach as I rocked back and forth slowly.

"Bend over a little more, baby girl. Let me see how well you take this dick."

I moaned and pressed my forearms to the bed between his legs. Lifting up, I stroked him with my body, taking my time, enjoying the pressure. His strong hands gripped my ass tightly as he massaged me.

"It's almost too much," I panted against my fist as I closed my eyes. Everything about him turned me on. His body was exactly the type that had me wet with nothing more than a quick glance. Strong muscles lined his lithe frame covered in tight tanned skin. The dark hair that dusted his chest and ran down to encircle his package was beautiful. He was model material, and yet I knew him when he wasn't.

"It's not too much." He patted my ass and repositioned himself to move up behind me.

I shifted and glanced back. "You look so good."

His smile said he already knew how good he looked. "Yeah? Like what you see, hmm?"

"Tease." I turned back around and pressed down on his dick, impaling myself on the thick bastard. A moan started that quickly turned into a scream as he gripped my hips and thrust hard. Whatever spot deep inside of me he was beating against, I wanted more of it. A lot more. "Don't stop."

He leaned over the top of me and cupped my breast with one hand while pressing his fist into the bed beneath us with the other. "No worries there, Bailey. I'm not going to stop until you beg me to. You're going to come all over me, and then you're going to take this big dick... nice and hard, angel."

"Please?" I whimpered and gripped the sheets as the world blew apart all around me. Every inch of my skin was covered in goosebumps as I released myself to the intensity of pleasure he forced upon me.

"Shit." I sat up in bed, my body shaking, my panties ruined. "No way. Really? I haven't seen him in years and-"

And I was dreaming of what he might look like and had been for the last ten years. Why he was my favorite wet dream was no mystery at all. The man was a god. I wanted him in my bed more than I wanted anything else in the world, but we were friends. Sort of.

He was Rhys's best friend. That had to count for something. I could get my hormones under control and get over this mild obsession.

"Okay, major obsession." I reached over and grabbed my phone to check the time. Seven a.m. Not the optimal time to get up on a Friday, but it would give me a chance to work out before heading into work.

I sat up on the edge of the bed as my body ached for the remnants of my dream. Would I see him again? Would he come back into the restaurant now that he knew I was there?

No. I was being an idiot. He was still in love with Laila, and no one would ever compare to her. I wasn't going to try to. It was unfair for all of us involved, and where some random-ass woman might steel him away from Laila's memory in the future, it wasn't going to be me.

We'd known each other most of our lives. I was Rhys's little sister. Nothing more.

———

"What? Seriously?" Ellen leaned against my counter later that night after work. "You didn't tell me you had a hottie firefighter from your past."

"He was in the Air Force for the first four years after high school." I smiled and went back to cutting carrots for our salad. I was beyond tired, but Ellen had to come over for our Friday late night dinner. It was getting to be a tradition even though we'd only started it a few months before.

It was nice to have a friend. One friend.

"Why did he get out of the service?" She moved over to the stove and dumped a handful of raw chicken into a hot skillet.

"He was on a diving trip, and something got in his eye. He didn't realize that it was a jellyfish tentacle until it had damaged his vision a little." I tossed the salad and turned to face my Friday night date. "What?"

"Is he... blind?"

"So what if he is?" I popped a cherry tomato in my mouth.

"Does he wear a patch?"

I laughed. "He's not a pirate, Ellen."

She snorted. "Why is it hot that he might *look* like a pirate?"

"Because you're a very sick woman. You need help. Obviously." I rolled my eyes and handed her a small bowl of salad. "He's beautiful."

"Like feminine?" She crinkled her nose. "I thought you like big strong guys."

"I do." I moved over to the fridge and got out a few different salad dressings. "He's huge. Much bigger than he was back in high school."

"Like muscles or a big dick, cause you know what they say..."

"That sugar is bad for you?" I smirked and handed her the sweetest dressing in my fridge.

"Ugh. Seriously?" She swatted my hand away. "Big muscles usually mean a little pecker."

"Pecker? Did you really just call it that?" I put the sweet dressing up and pulled out something more savory. "And just so we're clear, I didn't see his dick back then, and he certainly didn't whip it out at the restaurant the other night."

"Shame." She let out a huff.

"Agreed." I grabbed a fork and walked over to the kitchen table. After dropping down and squirting dressing all over my salad, I glanced up to find her watching me. "What are you thinking? I hate that look on your face."

"You should ask him out."

"He's half-blind."

"So what. He sounds dreamy."

"He wears a fucking eye patch." I was a horrible liar. I laughed the minute it came out of my mouth.

"He does not. You're so dumb." She walked over and sat down beside me. "Don't let me forget about the chicken."

"Fine." I poked at my salad. "Seriously though, I've had a crush on him forever, and then he just shows up at the fucking restaurant."

"What was he doing there?"

"He was on a date."

"Tell me more." She wagged her fork around and sang one of the tunes from the movie Grease. "Tell me more."

"You're single for a reason." I shook my head. "The girl he was on the date with had to have been in her early twenties."

"You're in your early twenties."

"Right, but she was like young-looking."

"Wait. Hold up." She lifted her hand in the air. "How old is this hottie?"

"He's in his early thirties. He's six or seven years older than me." I got up and walked into the kitchen to deal with the chicken. "He's honestly my prince charming."

"Does *he* know this?" Ellen turned and gave me a quirky smile.

"Of course not." I glanced over at her. "I'm his best friend's little sister."

"Okay. That's hot." She turned, got up and walked to the living room. "Keep talking. I'm just admiring your fucking awesome painting in here."

"His wife died a few years back, and he has a little boy that's probably around five now." I pulled the skillet off the stove and walked into the living room. "He's still very much in love with his wife, or so my brother says."

"So your brother still talks to the hottie?" She glanced over her shoulder and smiled. "Were they ever lovers?"

"What? No." I moved up beside her. "They were good friends. Best friends."

"And you were in love with him?" She glanced over at me.

"Still am." I shrugged. "But I'm not sure why. It's not like anything is going to ever come of it. Rhys, my brother, told me that Jeremy's mother is insanely strict and right up in the middle of his life. It's not like she would ever accept someone like me."

"Because why?" Ellen turned to face me and put her hands on her hips. "You're perfect. Like top of the charts perfect."

"Right." I glanced over at my painting. "A waitress that manages restaurants and spends her time dreaming of being a painter one day. I'm just an incredible catch for sure. No brains, barely any courage and a big ass to boot."

"Men love that ass." She shook her head and moved around. "And that painting is incredible. You're too down on yourself. It gets on my nerves."

"Up yours too." I studied the painting, seeing all of the things that were wrong with it instead of any of the things that were right. "Jeremy is the man I want in my life and my bed, but it's not going to happen."

"Why is that?"

"Because he sees me as a little sister, as a friend."

"He didn't hit on you the other night?"

I turned and walked back to the table, smiling at the memory of him pulling out his moves. "He did until he realized who I was."

"And then?" She sat back down and patted the table close to her. "Take off a load. Seriously."

"Then he went back to being sweet and kind."

"A man can't be sweet, kind and sex you up at the same time?"

"I don't know." I reached over and picked up the card from the guy at the art museum. "Maybe I should just give Edward a call. He seemed nice, and I don't know him at all. It would be a fresh start, you know?"

"Instead of overcoming years of yearning for someone and not getting them?"

"Exactly." I dropped the card. The very idea of having dinner with Edward left me cold, but it did seem like the right choice. Jeremy had too many ghosts that he carried around, and I wasn't going to be another one of them.

"New topic." Ellen took a bite of her salad and gave me a stern look. "When are we sharing your art with the world?"

I snorted. "Never."

"Virgin." She rolled her eyes. "In all ways."

"Hooker head. In one way." I laughed as she playfully jabbed at me with her fork.

"Call money bags. Go on a date and be miserable."

"It might be great."

"His balls probably rub his knees." She shook her head and stuck out her tongue.

"Maybe I like to be tea-bagged from up high." I poked at the chicken on the plate between us.

"Ugh. Gross." She pushed her plate away and leaned back. "It's Edward or your hot pirate with big muscles."

"Somehow Edward feels far more safe."

"Duh... He's not a firefighting pirate. Anything is safer than that."

"True." I turned my attention back to my dinner, ready to be done with the conversation. Jeremy wasn't going to be mine. Not ever. The best I could hope for was a friendship. It would be a start, and hopefully, I would be strong enough to be happy with nothing more than that.

I could love him from a distance.

I'd been doing it my whole life.

7

JEREMY

It had been a long two days since seeing Bailey in Blackhouse Grille. The shock of coming face to face with Rhys's little sister and finding her everything I wanted tucked beneath me in a set of cold sheets was sobering. Maybe my love life wasn't over.

"No," I growled and got up from the porch swing on my mother's big plantation-looking mansion. It was an odd style of home to have in the northeast, but she was a southern girl at one time. I started for the door only to stop short. Nina walked out wrapped in a shawl.

"How can you stand it out here? It's mid-Nov. It's fucking freezing."

"You kiss your momma with that mouth?" I turned and headed back to the porch swing. My sister was my best friend outside of Rhys, and I usually took every advantage to spend quality time with her.

"Hell no. You know Mom doesn't show affection." She chuckled, and I joined her.

"Mom's an odd duck, but she's ours." I dropped down on the swing and wrapped my arm around my sister's narrow shoulders as she sat down next to me.

"This is true." She glanced over at me, and I couldn't help but notice the worry in her eyes. "Did you talk to her yet, Jer?"

"About?" I feigned ignorance. It was my go-to when I wanted to avoid a conversation, but Nina knew what I was up to.

"About you dating and how it's none of her damn business who you go out with." Her expression tightened.

"Nope. And I'm not going to." I shrugged and pulled my arm away from her. "She's my momma. If she wants to set me up with a million sluts and gold diggers, then so be it."

"And crazy witches, and infantile looking women and-"

"The list goes on." I smirked and pressed my forearms to my thighs. "I'm the one on the dates. Believe me, the list goes on and on. Some of them are pretty funny stories." I let my head drop as a smile lifted my lips. The last two years of my dating life had been something of a reality TV show, and yet... I was still alone.

Nina rubbed the top of my back and let out a sigh. "I just wish she would leave you be. Maybe it's not time for you to find someone. You know?"

I wanted like hell to agree, but I couldn't. "Mom knows what she's doing, Nina. If she didn't push me, I'd become a bachelor and never date another woman."

"Why?" She moved up so we could see eye to eye. "You don't want to love again?"

"Hell no." I sat up and lifted my arms to stretch. "I don't want to do anything again."

"Hurts too much?" My sister leaned back and pulled her legs up. She wrapped her arms around her bent legs and pressed her cheek to her knee. "You still think about Laila all the time?"

"I dream about her every night." I glanced up toward the ceiling. "I see her in crowded areas and if I close my eyes and listen closely," I paused as tears burned my eyes, "I can almost hear her whispering my name."

"Oh, baby. I'm so sorry." Nina dropped her legs, moving closer and wrapped me in a side hug. "I didn't mean to upset you. Forgive me."

"It's all good." I forced my emotions back into the tight little box in the center of my chest where they belonged. Losing my everything left me shattered in a way that I couldn't contemplate coming out of. Not ever. No matter how many dates I went on.

"New subject. How's Rhys? Have you talked to him lately?"

"Yes." I reached up and pressed my fingers to my eyes as Nina moved back. "He's coming up here for Thanksgiving in a few weeks."

"Oh yeah?" I could hear the playfulness return to her voice. "Is he dating anyone?"

"No, you cougar." I glanced over my shoulder and gave her a warm smile. "His little sister Bailey is here. I ran into her the other night."

"Oh Lord." She stood and pulled her shawl around her shoulders as she turned toward the yard. "That girl has been in love with you her whole life."

"She was a kid, Nina. I was her brother's best friend. Of course, she was in love with me." I crossed my arms over my chest and kept to myself that I hadn't dreamt of Laila since seeing Bailey two nights before. It was terrifying to even think about replacing my wife in my dreams, and yet I had. Bailey at the park with me, spread out on a blanket, laughing, smiling, loving me.

"And you were a really good looking kid." She glanced over and wagged her eyebrows at me.

"Oh, great. So I was good looking. Thanks a lot. Just kick me in the nuts when you're done tearing me down, yeah?"

"So dramatic." She rolled her eyes and walked toward the house. "You need to talk to Mom, Jer. Set her straight."

"You do it this one time for me, and I'll do it the next time."

She laughed before disappearing back inside the house. "Not a chance in hell."

"Exactly," I mumbled and let my thoughts fade back to my dreams the night before. As lusty as I wanted them to be, they weren't at all. They were sweet, soft, loving.

"I'm thinking you might be a stalker." My sister glanced over at me as we walked up to the Blackhouse Grille later that night. Mother had set me up on another fucking date, but Nina saved me by taking me out herself.

"What? I love this place." I reached around my sister and mimicked her voice. "You might be a stalker if you like a good steak and eat at the restaurant near your house more than once."

"Keep it up." She glanced over her shoulder and chuckled. "I know what you're doing. You can pretend with everyone else, but it's not going to work with me."

"Whatever. I'm not listening to your gibber gabber. Get in there. It's cold." I pushed at her back with my shoulder and walked in behind her. She dealt with the hostess as I glanced around the restaurant. Every cell in my body pulsed with the need to see Bailey. It was silly, but something about her sparked hope inside of me. Maybe it would just be a friendship, but I needed that more than anything anyway.

"She's at the bar." Nina sat down at the table we were shown to and smiled up at me. "Go get me a Bud Light in a bottle with a lime."

"What?" I glanced down at my sister and back up at Bailey, who had yet to notice me. "The waiter will-"

"Now, please." Nina pushed at my stomach softly. "Go. Get. Me. A. Beer. At. The. Bar."

"What are you, a robot now?" I smiled and turned toward the bar. "How did you know that was her?"

"She hasn't changed a bit." My sister snorted and glanced over her shoulder. "She's filled out, but she still looks like little Bailey down the street, Jer."

"No." I shook my head and headed toward her. "No, she doesn't. Not in the slightest."

The little girl with boy's clothes, pigtails, and mud all over her face was all but gone. The woman in front of me was stunning and left my body hard and aching like a mother fucker.

"Jeremy." She smiled and pressed her hands to the bar before looking toward my table. She leaned closer and whispered playfully, "Another date? Need help?"

I laughed and glanced over my shoulder before turning back to her. "No. My older sister."

"Nina?" Her eyes lit up.

"Yeah. She's saving me from another blind date Mother set me up on." I shrugged. "My mom wants me to move on."

"I think that's very sweet of her to stay involved in your life." She reached up and tucked a strand of dark hair behind her ears. I wanted so badly to see her hair down, to slip my fingers into it, to make love to her pretty pink lips.

"Sweet?" I forced a laugh. "Try again. It's a pain in the ass, but I love her too much to tell her to back off."

"Tell Nina to do it?" She offered before bending down to grab something from the counter below her. The white button-down shirt she wore opened just right. The muted pink bra she wore pressed her tits up, their creamy tops thick and beautiful. My cock pulsed in my jeans and pressed against the back of my belt.

Fuck me. She was everything I wanted. I hadn't thought about making love to a woman in ages, much less taking my time to explore her fully. I wanted quick and dirty so that it was over and I could get on with life. I didn't want anything soft, sensitive or loving.

"Like what you see?" She glanced up to find me half-drooling. Fuck.

"Yes. You're so beautiful." I sat down at the barstool closest to me. "I can't even find remnants of the little girl who Rhys and I tossed in the air or dragged around in the mud."

She laughed, and that girl showed up. "Really? I don't see anything but that girl when I look in the mirror."

My thoughts dove into the gutter without hesitation, as if the fuckers were waiting right there to go south. I could picture her in front of a full-length mirror in her bedroom, naked and sexy as fuck. My body tightened as my balls contracted. I could have come standing there talking to her.

What the hell was wrong with me?

"Anyway," I cleared my throat as she moved around, working while we stood there talking. "I need a Bud Light for Nina."

"Sure. No problem." She turned and walked back to the cooler. My eyes moved down to the thick curve of her ass. How many men had she been with? None. I wanted it to be none.

"Rhys said he was headed this way for Thanksgiving. Are you cooking or taking him out, cause you guys could join us if you wanted to. My mother and Nina always go way above and beyond."

She walked back to me and set the beer on the bar. "I'd like that. Both me and Rhys would like to see your little one, and it might be fun to catch up."

"Good. I'll send him the information. Or I could send it to you." I pulled out my phone and lifted it as if waiting on something from her.

"Sure." She gave me her number and smiled. "You know I could help you out."

My cock twitched. "How so?" I wanted to seduce the fuck out of her, but I knew better. This wasn't the usual lust and run situation, and that alone terrified some part of me.

"Just bring your dates here." She moved back and shrugged. The movement caused her breasts to bounce, stealing my attention like I was a fucking caveman.

"You want to see my dates?" I forced myself to pull my attention back to her eyes. They pulled me in so deep. My pulse spiked, and it felt warm all of a sudden.

"No, silly." She was so comfortable around me, and I was about to come myself and start panting. What the fuck was going on. "I can help you out if they're ugh. Just give me the signal or text me now that you have my number. I'll come over and cause a scene for you."

"Be my baby momma?" I asked before I could stop myself.

"The one you haven't paid child support too, you sorry, sorry mother fucker." She leaned forward and laughed.

I smiled so hard my face hurt. God, she was beautiful. "I like naughty words coming out of your mouth, Bailey."

She blushed. "Get outta here. I'm not falling for your tricks."

"No? Damn." I took the beer, feeling a little too confident. "So what are you going to want in return for helping me out? Nothing is free in this world."

She pressed her fingers to her lips, and I stifled a moan. I wanted her to suck on her fingers for me. Fuck that. I wanted her to suck on my fingers. God, I needed to get laid. Again. And fast.

"What do I want... What do I want..." She paused and glanced up, looking me square in the face. "I want you to be happy. That's all."

I nodded and gave her a wink. "Then it's a deal." I turned and walked back toward Nina, my heart hurting, my dick dancing and my world shifting just a little too much.

8

BAILEY

TWO WEEKS LATER

"Are you sure you don't need me to work tomorrow?" I stood in the doorway of the office at the back of the restaurant.

Tanner leaned back in his chair and studied me. "No. You've taken every holiday since coming to work here. Go have fun with your brother. He's coming in tonight from Illinois, right?"

"Yeah." Excitement fluttered through me. I couldn't wait to see Rhys, and yet there was a part of me that knew exactly *why* I was beyond thrilled to see my brother for a few days.

Where Rhys was, Jeremy would be too. There was no separating them.

"Alright. Get out of here. Go get him." Tanner waved me off. "Take a few days off. I'm serious."

"Okay. Fine." I turned and walked through the restaurant, looking for Ellen. She didn't have good ties with her family, and though I hadn't invited her to Thanksgiving for fear that she'd fall in love with my older brother. He was a playboy and a half, and the last thing I needed was for my *only* friend to get heartbroken, and it be partially my fault.

"Hey!" Ellen jumped out from behind the waitress counter.

"Shit!" I moved back and lifted my hands. "You scared me to death. Warn someone, please?"

"Okay, so here's the deal." She ignored my request and moved closer. Never one to mince words. "I have no one to spend Thanksgiving with, and I know your brother is coming into town, but tell me when we can have a meal together at least. I don't want to encroach on your time with Rhys, but I do want to see you."

I bit on my bottom lip and worked through my issues quickly. I couldn't leave her spending the holidays by herself. No matter what.

"Just come with us." I shrugged.

She yelped and bounced up and down, excitement all over her pretty face. "Are you sure?"

"Yes, but there are some rules." I put my hands on my hips, feeling far older than I was.

"Rules?" Her smile faded. "No. No rules. Not for the holiday."

"Yes, rules. No hitting on or flirting with Jeremy."

"The pirate?" She crinkled her nose. "He's not my type. He's too bulky, and he's your guy. I would never do that."

"No hitting on my brother." I lifted my eyebrow.

"What? Why not? What if we have chemistry."

I laughed. "You will most certainly have chemistry, but don't do it, Ellen. He'll break your heart and then you and I will have issues, and I don't want that. Not over a lay."

"What if it's the best lay of my life? I don't think you're really thinking this through." She moved up beside me and slipped her arm into mine. "What if your brother and I are soulmates? Do you really want to fuck that up for two people that you really love?"

"Well, no, but-"

"Exactly. I have a *rule* in my own life."

"Really?" I stopped and turned toward her. There was no fucking way she had any rules. She was the most anti-rule person I knew. Pantser 100%. Never looking left or right before she crossed the street. Probably didn't know what a condom was.

"Yes. If I'm going to allow a man to put a ring on it," she lifted her hand and wagged her fingers in my face, "then I have to try the merchandise at least three times."

"Eww!" I swatted her hand away. "We're talking about my big brother here. You're grossing me out."

"Just updating you on the Ellen way of life."

"You're weird." I walked to the hostess stand, grabbed my keys and stopped at the door to look back at her. "I'm going to get Rhys now. We're having Thanksgiving at Jeremy's mother's house tomorrow. I'll text you in the morning and Rhys and I can stop by and pick you up. That good?"

"Yes, and thanks, Bailey. Seriously. It's weird not having anyone to spend the holiday with."

"No problem. I would have missed you like crazy anyway if you had somewhere to go."

She surprised me by walking over and pulling me into a tight hug. "If you don't want me to hit on Rhys, I won't. Seriously."

Ellen was my brother's type through and through. He would lay a turd in my bed if I cock-blocked him with my bestie.

"No, it's okay. Just trying to protect you." I hugged her back.

"Well, don't. That's what condoms are for." She moved back, winked and bounded off.

I growled before grabbing my coat off the rack and slipping it on. It was getting cold outside, and winter had officially set in. There would be no playing football out in the yard this year for Thanksgiving, but maybe that was a good thing. Everyone was getting older anyway.

A smile lifted my lips as I thought about telling my brother and Jeremy that they were too old to throw around the ball. I'd likely get dragged through the mud. Verbally or physically.

It was the way of the world... at least it was in my world.

"Sis!" Rhys walked into the baggage area at the airport and spread his arms wide. "You look too thin."

"Hush." I moved into his arms and pressed my cheek to his strong chest as I closed my eyes. He was a huge part of my life growing up and had been my biggest supporter in my decision to move from Illinois, where our parents relocated too just after Rhys left for the Air Force. Mom and Dad were still down the road from him, but I'd made the call to move back to my childhood home in New Hampshire.

Funny how no one I grew up with was there anymore, but the places were familiar. It was home to me, and always would be.

"I'm serious." He moved back and gripped my shoulders. His strong jaw was locked, and his icy blue eyes moved around my face as if assessing me. "Are you eating?"

"Nope. Liquid diet." I popped him in the stomach and walked toward the exit. "Did you check anything?"

"Hell no. That's a waste of time." He wrapped his large arm over my shoulders and moved us to the exit. "I'm almost surprised Jer didn't come with you."

"I didn't invite him." I shrugged and pulled my coat tighter. "We've seen each other a few times over the last month or so, but nothing too regular."

"You still have the hots for him?" Rhys released me and laughed as I gave him a warning look.

"I was a young girl, and he was your best friend." I popped the trunk on the car.

Rhys shut it and put his bag in the backseat instead. "And your point is? All that shit is still the case."

I smiled and got into the car. "How are Mom and Dad doing?"

He got in and buckled up. "They're great, but they miss you. You sure you don't want me to pack you up in my duffle bag and take you back with me?"

"Not a chance." I buckled, started the car and pulled out of the parking lot. "I love it here. I hated it when we moved after you left for the Air Force."

"I know you did, but it worked out well for me and you." He reached over and squeezed my forearm. He was right. The whole family moved to stay close to him, which allowed most of my late teens and early twenties to be supported by my big brother.

"That's true." I patted his hand. "So I should warn you about my best friend, Ellen."

"She hot?" He tugged at his seatbelt and growled. The poor guy was huge. His head almost hit the top of my tiny Toyota, and his knees were pressed against the glove box.

"She's my best friend. Hands off." I gave him a quick glare and turned back to focus on the road.

"Okay. I'll stay away from her. You stay away from Jer." He leaned back and smiled. "Deal?"

"I don't want anything to do with Jeremy."

"Really?" He leaned forward, bumping his big egg-head. "Look at me and tell me that without smiling."

Fuck.

I pulled my lips down into a slight frown and turned my face, but kept my eyes on the road. "I don't want-"

"You're smiling. Liar." He leaned back and crossed his arms over his chest. "Ellen is mine. Period."

"What?! You haven't even seen her." I reached over and popped him in the chest as the warmth between us brought me back to life. I missed him so damn much. I missed relationships in general.

"You wouldn't have warned me about her if she wasn't a good looking woman. I know you, Sis." He turned and looked out the passenger window. "Have you and Jeremy slept together?"

"No! We barely talk. Jeez." I gripped the steering wheel tighter. "Just stop asking questions. I'm not dating or seeing anyone."

"But you want to."

"Maybe, but it's irrelevant. He's still torn to pieces over Laila, and he should be. They were perfect for each other." The lump in my throat was thick. A part of me hated just *how* perfect they were for each other. It was something that no woman would likely overcome with Jer. It just seemed impossible.

"And she's dead, Bailey." He turned his attention back to me. "And she's been dead for two years. He needs to move on."

"Well, his mom is trying to help with that," I said very matter of factly.

He laughed loudly, the sound not friendly. "By setting him up on random ass dates? No. She's hurting more than she's helping. I'm going to tell her that too when I see her."

"Don't start anything this week, Rhys. It's Thanksgiving, and we're guests."

"I know." He nodded and pulled out his phone. "I'm not going to be ugly or rude. You know me better than that. I'm going to talk with Nina and see what she can do."

"Jer's sister?"

"Yeah." He pulled the phone to his ear. "What are the plans? We going home tonight or eating or what?"

"Home. I was going to make you dinner."

"Invite your friend over. I'm going to invite Jer over. I want to see him."

"What? The house is a fucking mess. You can't just-"

My brother's voice cut me off. "Jeremy! Hey man. I'm in town." Brief pause. "Yeah, man. Flight was great. Hey, I'm headed over to Bailey's place. I'll text you the address. Get your ass over there. We'll grill out or some shit." Another brief pause where I could hear Jeremy responding. "No, man. Cancel that shit. Tell her you have diarrhea from eating your own cooking. Get creative, dude. What's the matter with you? Just lie and get your ass over to my sister's. See you in an hour. Later!"

"Really?" I groaned and pulled off the freeway. "The house is a mess and-"

"We'll clean it."

"I look like shit."

"Put on a new shirt and some jeans and chill. You're not interested in Jer anyway, remember?"

"I hate you."

"Lies."

"True." I sighed and pulled up to the apartment. "You start cleaning, and I'll find something to cook."

"Call Ellen. I'm not playing the third wheel."

"This isn't a date," I called after my brother as he bounded out of the car the minute I pulled it to a stop.

"I know... it's a double date," he called back.

Ugh. Fuck my life.

9

JEREMY

"Damn," I mumbled and walked back out to the garage. Austin glanced up and gave me a sweet smile.

"What's up, Daddy?" He stood and wiped his greasy hands on his jeans.

"Uncle Rhys is here. You remember him much?" I tossed a rag to him as I walked back toward my bike.

"Nope." He wiped his hands and knelt. "You think the bike will take much longer?"

"No. Why? You got a hot date?" I smiled as he crinkled his nose and gave me a look.

"Dad. I'm five. Girls are super gross right now."

I laughed loudly, loving the kid more than anything else in the world. "They're not going to be super gross in a few years."

"There's a party at Katie's house for her birthday tonight." He ignored my comment and moved us to what seemed to be a much more comfortable subject for him. "I really want to go."

"Katie by Granny's house?" I moved over to the bike and put my hands on my hips as I studied it. It was going to take a few more hours to finish fixing the damn thing, and after Rhys's call, I knew I didn't have the time. "The cute girl with blond hair."

He rolled his eyes. "She has cooties. Hello."

"This is true." I stifled my need to laugh again. He had on his *serious face* which meant 'no laughing.' Memories flooded my vision, and the site of Laila rocking him when we first brought him home almost crippled me. He had to miss her as much as I did, but the little guy was stronger than all the rest of us put together. Or he pretended to be.

"Can I go?" He wiped his hands on his pants and smiled. "We can finish this later this week. It's Thanksgiving week. We have time. No school!"

"True. Yeah. Sure. Go in there and change and I'll take you over to Granny's house." I watched him skip away before calling my mother. I needed a way to get over to see Rhys without upsetting Austin, and now I had it. There was such a thing as grace, or so it would seem.

"Jeremy? Everything okay?" My mother always sounded panicked when she picked up the phone with me. It was like she was expecting me to deliver the same kind of news I did when Laila died.

"Yeah, Mom. Austin wants to come over tonight for a party down at Katie's house. Rhys's in town, so it works out well unless you had something planned."

"Not at all. Bring me my baby, and you go have fun with your friend. Make sure you stay alert for women that might be a good fit for you and Austin. You know it's not just about you, Jeremy."

"Yeah. Thanks, Mom. We'll be there shortly." I got off the phone as quickly as I could and walked into the living room. I could hear Austin down the hall somewhere singing the happy birthday song. I smiled and stopped beside the various pictures lining the bookshelf in the living room.

The one of me and Rhys smiling, arms wrapped around each other as we got out of basic training and planned on ruling the Air Force was one of my favorites. Life had taken a crazy ass turn, but it was what it was. He was still in, and I was Captain of the fire department in town.

"Dad!" Austin bounded into the living room and lifted his eyebrow at me. "Do you think I should wear a coat?"

"It's freezing outside. Yes." I walked toward him, picked him up and tickled him all the way back to the bedroom. He was going to get to meet both Rhys and Bailey the next day at Mom's when we all shared Thanksgiving together.

Would he like Bailey?

Would she like him?

Why the hell did I care?

I wasn't sure I wanted to answer my own question, and regardless of the answer, I knew one thing for sure... I did care. A lot.

"Hey, buddy!" Rhys wrapped me in a tight hug as he flung open the door to Bailey's apartment. The smell of something garlicky slapped me in the face, and my stomach growled loudly. I realized I hadn't eaten more than a piece of toast all day. It was something I was horrible about doing since Laila died. Feeding my damn self.

"Hey, you." I hugged him tightly and glanced up to find Bailey watching us. Her hair was up in a ponytail, and once again, I lamented over not getting to see it down. It would have been a little too much to ask her to take it down. Too intimate and maybe a little weird of me.

She looked like a model. Her light pink dress hugged her breasts and flared a little at her hips. It was long sleeved, but the length of it brushed about mid-thigh on her. She had on designer winter boots and a pretty necklace. She looked like she was ready to go out for the night, not BBQ with friends.

"You've gotten fat." Rhys moved back and patted my sides, squeezing my ribs.

"Ouch! Fuck man. That's not fat. It's muscle." I reached up and rubbed his head. "Like your big, ugly head."

He laughed. "You've met my little sister, Bailey."

She joined us and offered me a smile that calmed me. She might have been unsure of herself, but she was hiding it like a pro. Fuck. Maybe it was me who was unsure. For the first time in a long time, I was nervous.

"Hey." I reached out and gripped her shoulders before leaning over and kissing her cheek. "You look beautiful."

I wanted to hug her so damn bad, to feel her pressed against me, but there would be no hiding the hard-on it would leave me with. She was invading my thoughts and my dreams more and more over the last few weeks. It was becoming an obsession of sorts, which fucked with me, so I did what I always did when I was freaked out. I stayed away from her.

No way she felt the same way I did. And I wasn't entirely sure how I felt, but I knew I wanted her something fierce.

"Thanks. My friend Ellen just disappeared into the bathroom. She's been waiting to meet you." Bailey moved back, turned and walked into the kitchen. My eyes moved down the back of her perfect body, and my dick pulsed a few times in my jeans.

"I saw that." Rhys popped me in the chest and gave me a look.

"Dude. She's beyond beautiful. You couldn't have fucking warned me when I went looking for her that she wasn't the little brat we picked on? What the fuck?" I narrowed my eyes and lowered my voice.

He laughed loudly. "I told you she had grown up. Idiot."

"Whatever." I followed him out on the patio where the grill was already going. The weather had dropped drastically, and I wouldn't have been surprised if we had a snowy Thanksgiving by the looks of things.

"You interested in my kid sister?" He closed the door behind us.

"No." I slipped my hands into my pockets and blew out. A cloud formed in front of me and lingered. "Yes. Fuck. I don't know. She does something to me, Rhys."

"I'd beat anyone else's ass, but you're like a brother to me. If you're interested in taking her out, I'd trust you to do that."

"No." I shook my head and glanced back over my shoulder to see her working in the kitchen. "I didn't know she was your sister the first time I saw her." I stopped myself from telling him just how much she turned me on. There would be no coming back from that. He might have been my best friend, but this was his only sister, and she was younger. There were limits to what I could say.

"No? She looks the same to me, man." He nodded toward the kitchen. "Can you grab me a plate to put these burgers on?"

"Yeah, sure." I opened the door and paused. "Want a beer?"

He lifted his. "Already got one. There's a six-pack in the fridge. Help yourself."

"Alright. Thanks." I closed the door behind me as a cute blonde walked out of the bathroom and gave me a look.

"You're the pirate, right?" She tilted her head and studied me.

"Hey! Ellen. This is Jeremy." Bailey jogged around the corner from the kitchen. Her cheeks were pink and eyes wide.

I laughed and extended my hand. "Pirate, hm? Not sure how to take that."

"She meant because you save booties." Bailey glanced at Ellen and widened her eyes farther.

It was comical.

Ellen responded, her voice slow as if she were trying to follow Bailey's every move. "Yes. That's what I meant?"

I laughed and shook her hand. "Well, nice to meet you, Ellen." I glanced over at Bailey, who was rather mortified. "I'm going to grab a plate and a beer if that's okay?"

"Oh yeah. Let me help you." She turned and walked into the kitchen.

"I'll be on the deck with your fine-ass brother." Ellen wagged her eyebrows at me and smiled before walking out on the patio with Rhys.

I walked into the kitchen and stopped short. I had to reach out to stop myself from plowing Bailey over.

"I'm so sorry." She rested her hands on my hips, the innocence on her face left me realizing that she wasn't aware of how intimate her grip was. "I told her about you being in the Air Force, and then we talked about why you were out and-"

She droned on, but I couldn't hear anything else but a soft hum.

The smell of dinner cooking and the site of her in her pretty pink dress made the world dissipate.

"I'm gonna kiss you." I reached up and cupped her pretty face.

"Wait. What?"

"Shhh." I leaned down and pressed my lips to hers as I pulled her fully against me. My cock pressed to her stomach, and she had to know how much she turned me on. There was nothing I could do more than show her.

Her moan lit me on fucking fire. I had to have her. Soon.

Now.

BAILEY

The kiss was like nothing I'd ever experienced. I'd had a few make-out sessions in my time, but Jeremy's lips were incredibly soft, and his kiss was hungry. The deep groan he let out had my nipples budded, my pussy wet and aching.

I pressed against him and slid my hands around to the top of his perfect ass. Tilting my head a little, I opened my mouth and coaxed his tongue to join mine in a slow, sensual dance.

Everywhere. I wanted him to touch me everywhere, to kiss me in every crevice and over every curve.

"Fuck," he whispered roughly as he broke the kiss. "I'm sorry. You just look so good here in the kitchen."

"No. Please don't be sorry." I lamented as he removed his strong hands from my face and stepped back. It would have been too needy to ask him not to let me go. I had too much pride, and I didn't want to end up hurt again.

"No, really. I shouldn't have-" he paused and searched my face with his warm brown eyes. Everything about him set my blood on fire and left my heart flipping over in my chest. "Pretend that didn't happen?"

"Yeah. Sure." I reached up and brushed my fingers over my lips before turning and walking back into the kitchen. "You needed a beer and a plate?" I changed my tone and shoved the need to cry down deep inside my chest. It was a mistake. He didn't mean to kiss me. He just fell into my arms, and his lips landed on mine. Right. Great.

"Yeah. And a plate?"

"The counter just beside the stove." I moved to the fridge without looking back. "Go check on Rhys and save him from Ellen, please? I'll bring you a beer in a second. I need to find the damn bottle opener."

"A bartender doesn't carry one with her at all times?" He was trying to soften the situation with misplaced humor.

"I manage the restaurant, but good try." I bent over and moved some shit around in the fridge until I heard him walk out. Tears burned my eyes as anger swelled in my stomach. What did I think? Something would come of us? He's been without a woman for two years or something crazy like that. Of course, he's lonely and wants a bedmate.

"Not me." I stepped back and put the beer on the counter to grab a paper towel. I blotted my eyes and forced myself to chill the hell out. Nothing was going to happen between us. Not back when we were kids, and sure as fuck not now. There were only a few people that could break my heart properly, and Jeremy Bennett was definitely one of them.

I needed some hope for a different scenario. I needed something to lean on to get through the next few days.

Edward.

Picking up Edward's card from the table and my phone, I texted him quickly to see if he might be free for an event at the museum or coffee over the next few days. His response was quick and positive.

Edward: I almost thought you forgot about me, Miss Wright.

Me: No. Just got busy with the holidays.

Edward: There's a midnight wine event tonight. Join me?

Me: Yes. What time.

Edward: How about I meet you at the doors just before midnight?

Me: Perfect. Black tie?

Edward: Come in anything you want. I'm sure you'll be beautiful no matter what.

Me: Thank you.

Edward: My pleasure.

I set the phone down and picked up Jeremy's beer. My hands were shaking from the high emotions flying around me. I'd yet to be *good enough* in a relationship with any of my previous boyfriends, and most of them physically reminded me of Edward, but emotionally, of Jeremy.

And things never worked out well.

Sucking my pride back down my throat, I walked out to the balcony and opened the door. Rhys, Ellen, and Jeremy were laughing about something Rhys had said.

"And then I tossed the damn phone in the lake." Rhys lifted the back of his hand and wiped his eyes. "It was the funniest shit ever."

"You did?" Ellen's eyes got wide.

I handed Jeremy his beer and moved over beside my brother, who wrapped a strong arm around me.

"Thanks, Bailey." Jeremy's gaze lingered a little too long before he turned to Ellen, leaving the moment awkward at best. "Yeah. My dad flipped his shit to find out that I pitched my cell phone over a girl."

"When did you realize that your ass was grass? Tell them." Rhys reached out and pushed at Jeremy's strong chest softly. "I love this part."

Jeremy glanced down at his beer and chuckled as if he were lost in the moment.

I could have so easily let myself love him. I'd been doing it for years, but the man I'd made him into over the long stint of time where I didn't see him wasn't the man he was today. And me pretending that prince charming existed wasn't fair. With the death of that hope came a wave of emotion I wasn't expecting, and honestly didn't want to process.

"I realized it the moment I chunked it. It was like... oh fuck. My dad." He glanced up at me as my eyes filled with tears again.

"Excuse me. Finish your story. Just need to check on a few things in the-" I let my voice fade as I slipped back inside and walked quickly to the kitchen. I'd been doing such a damn good job of keeping myself in check when he came into the bar. I played the friend, though I wanted to offer so much more. But the timing was off, and he was far too much man for me.

I flipped the burners off and made my way down the hall to the bathroom. The door closed behind me, and I locked it about the time a wave of real tears came. I turned on the faucet and sat down on the toilet to press my face into a towel. The sound of my brother banging on the door a few seconds later wasn't the relief I hoped it would be.

"Sis? You okay?"

"No," I croaked out. "Stomach problems. Must have been that stupid roadside sushi you made me eat."

"Oh fuck. Seriously?" His voice was caring and filled with worry. I hated to lie to him. "You want me to get rid of everyone?"

"Yeah. I'm sorry. Give them take home plates?"

"Will do. No worries. I'll get you some 7-Up and crackers ready."

"Thanks, Bubba." I pressed my face back against the towel and wished I were anyone but me. Ellen and Rhys might think I was truly sick, but Jeremy would know the difference. He had to.

"Well, don't you look beautiful." Edward offered his arm as I walked up to the front of the museum in a long, black dress and heels. I had my hair up in a bun and more jewelry on than I normally wore.

Thankfully enough, Rhys fell asleep on the couch at ten, giving me time to get ready and leave for my date. It was stupid to try to make two wrongs into a right, but I had committed and didn't want to look like a flake just in case.

"Thank you. You look very handsome tonight." I glanced up at him and smiled. He was incredibly good looking. Not my type, but still very attractive.

"These people are going to think you're my daughter." He chuckled as I slid my hand around his arm. "Let's give them something to talk about, right?"

"Absolutely." I walked in, and the room was filled with people. Dainty little white lights were strung all over the top of the main gallery, and a multitude of servers moved around with trays of champagne and different treats to try. "I love this place. It makes my heart sing."

He chuckled. "It's an intellectual paradise."

"Because there's no right way to interpret a painting, right?" I moved up to a new one that I'd yet to see in the gallery before. "It's really about how the art speaks to you, right?"

"No. Not at all." His tone was a little condescending. "It's about what the artist was trying to portray. It takes time to study and understand the art to really appreciate it. You can't just walk in and take it for what it's worth." He smiled down at me, though his lips were drawn a little tight. "It's immaturity. You'll learn to mature in your appreciation for the real meaning behind the mask. It takes time."

"Right." I nodded and turned back to the painting, feeling all of sixteen all over again. Not good enough. Not smart enough. Not enough.

"I'll be back in a few minutes. I want to mingle with a few people from City Hall."

"Sure." I glanced over my shoulder. "Do you want me to come with you?"

"Oh no. They know my wife. I would never in a million years hear the end of it." He gave me an incredulous look like I was a young, simple fool.

"Your wife?" I lifted my eyebrow.

"Of course, Bailey. Did you think a wealthy man like myself wasn't married?" Another slip in his tone to leave me feeling even more stupid than I apparently was.

"You're not wearing a ring." I glanced down and back at him as my stomach sickened.

"Of course not. How would I find a mistress with a ring on?" He smirked and nodded toward the crowd. "Wait here. I'll talk to a few more people, and then we can leave."

I turned back to the painting as horror ran through the center of my chest. The minute *Edward* was gone and I was alone, I took off for the door. Walking as quickly as I could, I made my way back to my car, tore my heels off of me and drove home feeling so pathetic. Much more than I did when Jeremy pulled away from me.

Why did I try? It seemed like a stupid, immature thing to do.

Especially when it never worked out before.

Never.

JEREMY

I moved around my mother in the kitchen the next morning and her and Nina bickered back and forth on the right temperature to put the oven on for the stuffing. They were getting louder and louder, both of them wrong and yet neither of them would ever admit it.

"Hey!" I stopped at the edge of the kitchen and lifted my hands. "It's 375 degrees. That's what Laila always did. One hour at 375 degrees and then put the broiler on to crisp the top, okay?"

My sister's brow softened as my mom's eyes filled with tears.

"No. No crying." I let out a sigh and walked across the kitchen to pull Mom in my arms. "It's okay."

"No, it's not. I hate the holidays with you not having someone to love you." My mom cried against my chest.

I gave Nina the death stare. "What about Sis, mom? She needs someone to love her."

"Nope." Nina smiled like the tomcat she was. "I'm unlovable, bossy and stubborn as hell. Just ask Mom." She tossed a dishtowel at me and walked out of the kitchen.

"She is horrible, right?" My mom moved back, bent over and grabbed the towel and wiped at her eyes. "No, she's just a crazy cat lady. It's nothing to be ashamed of. She needs to own it."

"I heard that!" My sister yelled from the living room.

I smiled at my mother. "Why do you let your chef's off during the holidays? You're going to wear yourself out in this damn kitchen. Come sit down and I'll call them back."

"No." She shook her head. "While your father was here, he was very adamant about not letting our staff work on the holidays. I'm not breaking that rule. I like it."

I nodded and moved up beside her to help as someone knocked at the front door.

Nina's voice rang out. "Jer. It's Rhys and Bailey."

"Who?" My mother glanced over at me. "He brought his sister? Why?"

"And some blonde chick that's bouncing on her toes." Nina's tone said that we were all in for a long day.

"That's Bailey's good friend, Ellen." I leaned over and kissed my mother's cheek. "Please be nice. I have one friend in the world, and he's at the door."

"He brings too many memories with him, son. You need to-"

"Leave it alone, Mom." I gave her a wink and walked out of the kitchen. Her bitching was soft, but I could still hear it. She hated me being around anyone that might pull me off the path she wanted me on. Rhys being a perpetual bachelor did *not* help the cause at all.

"There you guys are." I pulled the door open and smiled at my best friend before moving back. Bailey looked like a dream in the background, but her coloring was a little off.

"We got lost in the hedging, man. I always forgot that you rich people enjoy your bushes." He gave me a funny look.

I rolled my eyes before patting him on the back and turned my attention to his little sister as he walked in.

"Hey. You look like you're still a little under the weather." I nodded at Ellen as she moved into the house and introduced herself to everyone before I could do it for her.

"Just a long night." Bailey shrugged and moved around me with nothing more than a quick glance. Fuck. I knew better. I shouldn't have kissed her in the kitchen the night before, and yet all I could think about was doing it again. Everything about the kiss had been right. I was turned on from the moment it happened until later that night when I fucked myself for a good hour in the shower. For the first time since Laila and I started dating back in school, I moaned someone else's name. I was relieved and ashamed at myself.

Was I allowed to move on? What did that say about the way I loved her? About my devotion to who we were supposed to be?

"You're in your head. Get out." Nina walked past me and popped me in the chest. "And if you can't, I'm here for you."

"Thanks, Sis." I took a deep breath and followed everyone into the large kitchen my mother hated, but my father once loved. "Mom. Did you get to meet everyone?"

"I did." She turned back to the stove; her shoulders pulled in tight. She was less than happy that I'd invited anyone over for Thanksgiving seeing that it was supposed to be a *family event*.

"Awesome. Rhys grab some beers. Let's go into the media room and watch the game. Nina, grab some snacks from the fridge that we picked up?" I nodded and turned to Ellen and Bailey. "Alright, ladies. You need a grand tour?"

Ellen was much more excited than Bailey was. I needed to apologize again or something. I didn't want the dust settling between us and our relationship tanking because I couldn't keep my damn hormones under control.

"Yes!" Ellen moved up and slipped her arm into mine. "Bailey. Get his other arm. Let's check this place out."

"Sure," she said softly and slipped her arm into my other one.

Tingles ran up my arm. I glanced down at her and spoke softly. "You feeling any better?"

"Somewhat." She shrugged and nodded toward the living room. "Tour please."

"Yeah, sure." I walked them through the house and stopped at the media room to find Nina and Rhys laughing together. It was almost like old times. The only thing missing was Laila.

Ellen bounded across the room toward the big screen and yelled something that sounded like, 'Go Team!'

"Where did you find her?" I glanced over at Bailey.

A smile crept across her perfect lips. "She works with me at the restaurant. She's my only friend."

"Well, then I guess we'll keep her." I turned a little toward her and forced myself not to reach out. "Hey. About last night."

"It was nothing." She smiled up at me, and her expression stilled me. She was hurt. I wasn't used to dating or anything of the sort, but I'd seen the look on my wife's face too many times to ignore it. "Seriously. Odd moment. I thought maybe I would feel some spark, but it was just like kissing an old friend, or your grandmother."

I almost swallowed my tongue, but I flipped on my humor like I always did when someone stabbed me in the chest. "You've kissed my grandmother before?"

She laughed and shook her head, causing a few more strands of dark hair to fall from her ponytail. "You're too much."

"So get this," Rhys walked up and put his arm around Bailey's shoulders, "this crazy kid went on a date last night."

"It wasn't really a-" she started, but Rhys cut her off.

"Did you get dolled up for him?" Rhys asked.

"Yeah, but seriously, it wasn't-"

"Like long black dress, heels, and jewelry. It was a champagne affair at the art museum." Rhys snorted.

"Sounds like a great date. I want details." Nina moved up beside us and smiled at Bailey.

"I thought you were sick?" I asked as my mother walked in and cleared her throat. "Jeremy. Someone named Mayhem is on the phone from the station?"

"Oh yeah. Sure." I left the conversation, though I was more than curious to find out what the fuck happened between the time I kissed Bailey and the time she left to spend the night in another man's arms. My stomach soured at the thought as if it were any of my fucking business. It wasn't.

"Here you go." My mother tossed my cell to me.

"Thanks." I put it to my ear and made a beeline for the side door. Bailey dressed up and went on a date? Did she stay at the guy's house?

Who was he? What did he look like? What did he do? How old was the fucker?

Great. Now he was a fucker.

"Talk to me." I walked out onto the patio as a cold sweat rolled over me. What was I doing? She didn't belong to me, nor would she ever. She was off-limits, and I'd fucked up by simply kissing her the night before. I needed to watch myself.

"Hey, Cap. I know this is going to sound stupid, but the lady that was going to cook our Thanksgiving meal for tonight kicked the bucket this morning."

I stiffened. "Wait. What? Who died?"

"Jones' Gramma." He cleared his throat. "All these guys are stuck up here, and we got nothing to eat. I was going to leave and grab a few things cause I feel like shit about the old lady kicking the bucket, but that would leave the crew short. You know we're playing skeleton crew up here."

Mayhem was too much, and the bastard knew it.

"Yeah, no worries. I'll be there in thirty minutes with some food."

"You sure?" He sounded relieved.

"Absolutely. Just keep everyone's spirits up. I'll bring some stuff by and then head back home. Our dinner isn't for a couple of hours at least."

"Alright. Thanks, Cap." He dropped the call.

"Damn." I walked back into the house to find my mom and Bailey in the kitchen. Both of them looked a little tense.

"Hey. I gotta run up to the station and get the guys some food. Their plans fell through, and I hate to think they're working on a holiday without getting anything good from it." I glanced over at Bailey who looked like she needed saving. "You wanna ride up there with me? I could use an extra set of hands, and maybe you'll pick some good stuff for them. I'm thinking ham and bread."

She nodded. "Yeah. I can help."

"I can go with you, Jeremy." My mother started to pull her apron off.

Bailey lifted her hands and pressed them together like she was praying. Fuck. What had my mother said to the pretty girl?

"No, Mom. Seriously. I'll be back in an hour tops. You stay here and finish this beautiful meal you're making. Me and Bailey will run up there and be right back." I walked over and kissed my mom on the cheek as she stared me down.

"Fine. Don't be over an hour or our dinner will be ruined."

"No problem." I slipped my hands into my pockets and glanced over at Bailey. "You ready?"

"Sure." She walked past me quickly and made it to the front door before I could turn the corner.

Fuck. Mom had definitely said something to her... and it was probably credited to it being for my own good.

BAILEY

"*Y*ou *do realize that Jeremy isn't interested in anyone under the age of thirty, right? He's looking for a mother for Austin, not a part-time girlfriend to fix his male yearnings.*" Jeremy's mother's voice echoed in my head as I stepped out of the house.

"Hey. What happened in there?" Jeremy moved up beside me as we walked toward the road.

"Nothing." I shrugged and pointed to his bike. "Can we take your bike?"

"Yeah. You bet." He walked up to it and handed me a helmet. "You're going to have to take your hair down to get that thing to fit."

"Sure." I set the helmet down and pulled at the twist-tie holding my hair together. It cascaded down my back and over my shoulders before I could get my fingers in it to make it behave a little. The lust in his eyes burned me. "What?"

"I love it." He reached out and slid his fingers into my hair, gripping it a little and making a sound that left me thinking about how far I wanted his kiss to go the night before.

"Good. No touching please." I pushed at his chest. The strong muscle of his pectoral gave little as I pushed harder and smiled. "Stop. Seriously. We're just friends, remember?"

"Yeah, well, I was thinking about pushing our friendship a little more each time I saw you, but it would seem that you already have a guy in your life. A rich one, no doubt." He got on the bike and offered me his hand. "Right?"

I put the helmet on, ignored him and got on the back of the bike. What he didn't know wouldn't hurt him. A laugh bubbled up in me as he growled. I wrapped my arms around his waist and leaned closer. The position let me press my breasts against him and tuck myself against his strong back. My panties were going to be ruined by the end of the day, but Jeremy was around -- what else was new.

We drove to large grocery store and parked near the front. It was freezing outside, but my thoughts kept me warm enough. Jeremy pulled off his helmet and offered me his hand.

"Are you really not going to tell me about this guy?" He released my hand and took my helmet.

"What's there to tell?" I snorted and walked toward the store.

He caught up. "Who is he? What does he do? Fuck. How old is he?"

"You don't really care to know all of this. We're friends, Jer." I grabbed a cart and leaned over, walking in front of him. I glanced back to find him eye-fucking the hell out of me. "Right?"

"I don't know." He moved up beside me and adjusted himself. "My dick wants us to be a whole lot more than friends."

I rolled my eyes and glanced over. His cock was thick and hard, pressing against his jeans. I wanted to be playful, but it was far too fine for that. "Too bad I'm not into love 'em and leave 'em. Sorry. I'm not that girl." I turned back around and walked toward the bakery.

"Are you and this guy serious?"

"No." I left the buggy and picked up a few items as I tried to ignore the incessant beating of my heart. The man just behind me held hostage every wicked fantasy I'd ever had since I was fifteen.

"No?" He moved up beside me. "That's all?"

"Yeah." I lifted the two cupcake trays up. "Do firefighters like cupcakes?"

"We eat anything." He growled and took the trays from me. "Tell me about him, Bailey. You need someone to protect you."

"I have a brother already, and honestly, your dick comment is really disturbing if you're not trying to play big brother to me." I walked back to the cart, playing it as smooth as I could. I was actually pulling it off. A giggle rose deep inside of me at the realization. He, on the other hand, wasn't pulling anything off.

"Bailey." He put the stuff in the cart and moved to stand beside me. "Look at me."

I turned and lifted my chin. "There is nothing to tell. He was richer, smarter, older and much more put together than me."

"Lies." He tilted his head a little and seemed to be struggling not to reach out and touch me.

I wanted him to so fucking bad. Needed him too. To feel his hands on me again would have been bliss. It could have righted the wrongness of the kiss the night before. Not the kiss. Him pulling back from the kiss.

"He was looking for a young mistress, and I played right into his hands." I shrugged as my facade dropped a little. "I don't know why I thought a guy like him would be interested in a simple girl like me." I reached out and pressed my hand to the center of his chest, forcing him to step back a little. "I mean... you weren't interested in me after our kiss last night either, and you know me." I forced a laugh before leaning back over the cart and pushing it toward another aisle.

"Bailey. That's not true." He gripped my arm, pulling me back against him. The firm press of his chest against my back was almost too much.

I closed my eyes and let out a soft whimper as my heart twisted in my chest. "Please don't."

"It's not true." He leaned over and brushed his lips by my ear as his strong hand slid around to press flat against my stomach just under my breasts. "I'm just damaged goods. I don't want to drag you into a lusty night of sex and leave you with the idea that-"

"That I'm good enough for more than a few nights." I pulled his hand away slowly as to not make my emotions too obvious. "I get it. Thank you for that."

"Bailey."

"This conversation is over." I glanced back and narrowed my eyes a little. "Seriously. Back off with it."

He lifted his hands. "Can I explain?"

"No," I barked and turned, swallowing my tears back down. Why had I decided to go to the stupid Thanksgiving at his mother's house? She couldn't stand anyone she didn't pick for Jeremy. Rhys had told me that a million times in a bitch-session growing up. Funny enough, Jeremy's mother hadn't picked Laila. She hadn't even liked her. "What else do you want to get?"

"Something for dinner for the guys." He moved up beside me, his hands in his pockets and eyes forward.

"Let's get turkey and stuffing from the deli?" I forced my tone to lighten. I paused and turned toward him. "I don't want to fight with you. I don't want this tension between us. The kiss was a mistake. Whatever the reasons are behind that, let it go. Seriously."

"And if I can't?" He pulled his bottom lip into his mouth.

My hormones stood up and screamed for attention. "Then I guess that's your problem. I'm not like most girls."

"Tell me more about this asshole who Rhys and I are going to beat to a pulp tonight."

I laughed. "No. He's an idiot for thinking that I was a whore."

"I'm gonna kill him." He moved past me, his shoulder brushing by my back. Even the slightest touch felt so good. "He didn't touch you, did he?"

"Nope. He didn't even kiss me and run." I smiled as he glanced back and gave me a stern look.

"Not funny."

"I thought it was." I leaned against the cart and studied the way his ass filled up his jeans. I wanted my hands all over that ass, squeezing and scratching as he made love to me long into the night.

"I don't like it." He turned around and lifted his eyebrow. "Were you checking me out?"

"Yes. I have a pulse, and every other woman in this place is checking you out." I turned back to the cart. "You're very handsome, and I'm sure you know it."

"It doesn't do me any favors." He stopped beside me and pressed his chest against my arm, his nearness delicious.

I glanced up at him but didn't move. "No, your mother doesn't do you any favors."

"I wanna kiss you again so fucking badly, but I think we'd get carted off to jail if I started something in here. There's a law against indecent exposure."

I snorted. "I'm not sleeping with you. It's forbidden. My brother would kill us both, and I'm not interested. You're hot. So what. A lot of guys are."

"And do you want to sleep with me?" He ran his fingers down the back of my hair, sliding each digit in and out of my silky locks.

"Do you snore?" I moved away and pushed the cart down another aisle. I wasn't going to survive him. He was hot and cold. Ready and not. It was more than I could take, so I did what I always did when I wanted something and couldn't have it.

I faked it until I could make it.

13

JEREMY

"Hey. Thanks for going with me." I stepped back from the bike as Bailey pulled her hair back up into a ponytail. The thought of it not being down wanted me to stop her, but I'd overstepped my boundaries way more times than I should have.

"Sure. No problem." She turned as Austin's little voice filled up the space around us.

"Daddy!" He bounded down the stairs, his little arms wide and short legs racing toward me.

I laughed and bent down to pick him up. "You finally up from your nap?"

"Yeah. I didn't even know I fell asleep." He smiled down at Bailey. "Who is *this?*"

His heart pounded in his chest so hard that I could feel it against my chest. His eyes were wide, and if I didn't know any better, I'd have thought he was smitten with Bailey. Not that I could blame him in the slightest.

She was everything I wanted in my life when I let myself dream a little again. Fuck me for trying to seduce her. She deserved more than a quick fuck and run. So did I.

"This is Uncle Rhys's baby sister." I winked at Bailey and helped Austin down out of arms.

He glanced up at me and smiled. "She's pretty like mommy was."

His word hit me square in the chest. "Yeah. She is, right? I think she can hear us, though."

Bailey laughed softly before kneeling in front of him. "Your name is Austin?" He nodded and moved closer to me. "And how old are you?"

I brushed my hand over his head and watched the beautiful creature entice him to open up. I wanted more than I should have with her, and I knew myself... it was going to start with sex. It was the easiest way to show her how much she turned me on - physically, emotionally, mentally.

Rhys was going to fucking kill me.

"I'm five." Austin took a step away from me and touched Bailey's earring. "Is this a Mockingbird?"

She glanced up at me with a question in her eyes. "I think so. I can't see it."

He giggled. I smiled and nodded. "They're Mockingbirds. They look really pretty on Miss Bailey, don't they, Aus?"

"Yes, Sir." He turned to face me. "Dinner is ready. Granny is in her room resting. She overdid it." He took off and raced up the stairs while he called over his shoulder. "Miss Bailey. You can sit by me at dinner."

"Okay." Bailey turned to me. "God, he's so cute. Like the perfect mix of you and Laila."

I smiled and reached out, gripping her arm carefully before sliding my fingers down to her hand. I pulled her a little closer to me.

"What am I gonna do about this thing building inside of me, Bailey?"

"What thing?" she whispered softly and pressed her free hand to my chest.

I trapped my hand over hers. "This thing you're doing to me."

She smiled and glanced toward the house. "You're going to man up and ask me out on a date, or you're going to let your mom keep setting you up with horrors."

"Wait. Whores?" I lifted an eyebrow and released her.

"Horrors. With an 'H'." She snorted, and I smiled. Fuck me she was beautiful.

"Go out with me." I reached for her hand again.

"Maybe." She tugged her hand back. "My brother's watching from some odd window shutter, I promise. Don't ruin your friendship over me. You both need each other too much."

"You don't think he would be okay with something starting between us?" I wanted to press the point. Shit. I wanted to press up against her. Worship every inch of her sexy little body. Fuck her against every wall in my house and make her cry out my name until she was shaking and covered in come.

A growl rose in my chest. My lust had been lukewarm since Laila at best but now was different. So damn different that it hurt.

"I'm not sure." She took a step back as I took a step closer. "But I'm not going out with you until you talk to my brother."

I glanced down at my dick as the fucker danced around, pulsing with a painful sensation. "Well, you go in and entertain while I try to get rid of what you do to me."

"Just because yours is obvious doesn't mean that you're the only one feeling anything." She moved close enough to brush the back of her fingers down my dick, playing with me.

"Shit." I closed my eyes, gritted my teeth and gripped her hand tightly. "I'm not a soft guy in the bedroom. If you say yes to dinner and a walk around the park, know I'm gonna try. Period."

"I would be pretty upset if you didn't." She pulled her hand free and turned toward the house. "Come on. You have to talk to Rhys, and I have a little boy to entertain before dinner."

I smiled. "Sounds like you have the easier of the two things to deal with." I walked to the house, readjusting myself. What was I going to do with her? Make love to her, yes. So hard and long and sweet that she yearned for me when I wasn't around. The old desire to make someone fall so deep in love with me that she couldn't stand a moment away from me roared to life inside of me.

It stole my breath.

"Maybe there's hope," I whispered and patted my chest as I followed a little ways behind her.

She was in the kitchen with my mom, Nina and Austin by the sounds of their voices, but Rhys and Ellen were still in the game room, or so it seemed. I made my way down there and poked my head in.

Rhys glanced toward me and smiled. "What's up, brother? You didn't leave Bailey with those heathen bastards at the fire station, right?"

"Nope. She's in the kitchen with little man." I took a deep breath. "Can I talk with you for a minute?"

"Yeah. Sure." He got up, and I realized that Ellen's legs were in his lap. "Be right back, pretty girl."

"Hurry back, please." She smiled at him and turned back to the TV.

"What's that all about?" I asked as we walked down the hallway to my old bedroom.

"It's just sex. We're going to fuck until I leave and that's it." His tone was so nonchalant.

"You're such a whore." I walked into my room, dropped down on the bed and glanced up at him. "So I need to talk to you about Bailey."

He laughed and closed the door. "I'm not her daddy, Jer."

"I know, but you're my best friend, and she's your baby sister." I clasped my hands together. "I don't even know how to start this. I don't know where I fully want things to go with her."

"Sure you do." He crossed his arms over his chest and leaned against the closed door. "You're just scared as fuck to admit it."

I nodded. "Yeah. That's actually spot on." I reached up and pinched my bottom lip between my thumb and middle finger. "I don't want to fall in love, but I could see it happening so easily with her."

"Which is most likely going to happen. Let's see why." He lifted his fingers and ticked off each with his reasonings. "She's beautiful. She's young and vibrant. She's totally mother material. You trust her because you know her and lastly-" He lifted an eyebrow as if waiting for me to give him the final reason.

"She's loved me her whole life." I cupped my hands over my face and flopped back on the bed. "Can you imagine what Laila would say about me being interested in your little sister?"

He laughed from across the room. "No, and you probably wouldn't want to hear it, but dude-"

"I know." I sat back up and stared my closest friend in the face. "Don't say it. Please."

"I have to Jeremy." He let out a long sigh and glanced around. "Laila is gone, man. She's been dead for two years, and where I'd trade my life for hers to give her back to you, it ain't happening."

"I know." I leaned over a little as all the air seemed to be sucked from the room. "Two years," I whispered as pain wrapped around my chest and squeezed with all its fucking might. "And I'll never get over losing her, Rhys."

"And you shouldn't." His hand ran down my back as he dropped down next to me. "But, it is time to move on. You have a great girl waiting for that opportunity. She's been waiting a long ass time."

"And you're okay with that?" I glanced up at my best friend as I beat back tears. Nothing kicked me in the nuts as hard as remembering mine and Austin's loss. It was so goddamn unfair.

"Oh yeah. Let Bailey help you heal, brother. Let her into your heart, and she'll clean house." He rubbed my back harder. "She'll respect the fact that you'll never let Laila go, but be sure of your intentions before you invite her in, Jer. She's a good woman and deserves a really good man."

"That kicks me out." I snorted and tried to force a smile.

"No, it puts you first in line." He gave me a strong hug from the side. "Just realize that she's not looking for a one-nighter or even a one-yearer."

"I get it." I nodded toward him. "I'll figure this out. I just wanted you to know that I was interested."

He laughed and stood up. "Good. It's about damn time. Now, let's go eat dinner and watch the rest of the game. All this moving around bullshit on Thanksgiving isn't good for anyone."

"Who told you that?" I stood and followed him out, feeling much better.

"No one. I just made it up so we can watch the game and chill after dinner."

"That's what the plan was anyway." I patted his back and moved around him into the kitchen. Bailey had Austin on her hip and was letting him stir the gravy on the stove. The moment caught me off-guard, but in a really good way.

"And if you're careful and just move it side to side, it will never spill," Bailey explained to my son.

"I like it." Austin laid his hand on her shoulder. "I like you too."

"Awww... I like you too." She kissed his forehead as I walked up.

"And what about me? Am I just chopped liver?"

"Ewww... I hate liver." Rhys walked in and moved up to the stove. "Let's do this thing. I'm getting hangry."

I took Austin from Bailey as she, Mom and Nina plated everything up. "Someone get this man a Snickers. He's turning into a Diva."

"Turning into?" Bailey walked by with a bowl of mashed potatoes in her hands. "He has *always* been a diva."

"This woman speaks the truth!" Rhys declared, and we all shared a good laugh. It felt good. Right. Like coming home.

BAILEY

"You don't have to do that." Jeremy moved up beside me at the sink as I washed the dishes with Nina from dinner.

"You hush your mouth," Nina quipped playfully. "It's hard as shit to find good help."

"I like it." I tried to blow a strand of wayward hair out of my face.

"Here. Let me help you." He reached up and tucked it behind my ear.

"Thanks," I responded softly as my heart fluttered in my chest. What the hell was happening between us? He wasn't just *some* guy. He was *that* guy. He was Rhys's closest friend and the one I'd been thinking about, dreaming about, yearning for most of my life. No matter how wrong it seemed, I'd always wanted Jeremy Bennett.

"Here. You take over please. I'm going to head home. Austin is going with me." Nina moved back and grabbed a dry towel. "Mom is already passed out. Ellen and Rhys are in the game room enjoying the game. You guys have fun and just make sure you lock up before you leave."

"Will do. Thanks, Sis." Jeremy gave his sister a quick hug and moved up beside me. "I'm going to pretend to wash these dishes, but you really do all the work. That seem good to you?"

I laughed. "You're just full of funnies, aren't you?"

"If we're being honest, I haven't much felt like being full of anything good in the last two years." He licked the side of his mouth and pressed his hand to my lower back. "And then three weeks ago, I walk into the restaurant with a crazy red-headed witch child that my mother set me up with-"

I laughed loudly.

"Right?" He smiled and slid his hand over my back to my hip, gripping it as he moved closer. "And the most beautiful girl I've seen in a long ass time was at the bar."

"Was she the one you hit on thinking she was someone else?" I smiled and slid my hands into the soapy water to rinse them off.

"Oh yeah." He leaned over and pressed his forehead to the side of my head. The warm sensation of his breath against my ear had my toes curling. "I was stunned. Shocked into silence by your beauty."

"You were quiet is all if I'm remembering it right." I turned to face him and slid my wet hands up his t-shirt before locking them behind his thick neck.

"Hey. Who's telling this story?" He ran his hands over my hips to my ass and caressed me as he pulled me closer. "I was silent."

"Fuck," I mumbled as lust twisted in the center of my stomach. "Please don't start something you're going to regret later."

"Hush." He pressed his forehead to mine. "I didn't regret the kiss, Bailey. I wanted so fucking much more than that kiss. I was worried you might regret it."

"You've lost your mind. I've waited for this day for most of my life." I pulled him down as I lifted to my toes. My kiss was hungry and aggressive.

He gripped the back of my neck with one hand and cupped my ass tightly with the other. His tongue rolled past mine as he made love to my mouth and dominated every second of our kiss.

"My room. Now." He nipped at my lips and moved back. He turned me around and popped my butt. "Move it, or my mother is likely to walk in on us on the floor."

"Jeremy." I walked toward the hallway. "I don't-"

"No. Stop. No more talking." He gripped my shoulders tightly and moved me down the hallway.

My heart thundered in my chest. I needed to tell him that I'd never been with anyone fully. Lots of oral sex. No, scratch that. I wasn't saying *that* shit. Maybe I could just go with it and he would never know.

"Here." He pulled me flush against him and pressed his hand to my stomach again. He reached out and opened the door with his free hand as he leaned down and whispered into my ear, "Feel how hard you make me? Like my cock is going to crack the fuck in half. This isn't the first time, Bailey. I ache for you, baby."

I whimpered and reached back to grab his thighs. I didn't care who was around. I wanted him above me, below me, deep inside of me. The fear of what might happen dissipated as he moved us into his room.

Greedy hands pulled my shirt off and worked me out of my bra so quickly I couldn't keep up.

"Tell me you want this. Tell me you want me." He pressed me to the door and moved down, his lips and tongue worshiping my breasts one at a time. I glanced down to see him pull my dark pink nipple deep into his mouth. The sight and sound of him lost to ecstasy was one of the most beautiful things I'd ever seen. I wanted to memorize it just in case I never got the chance to see it again.

"I want you so bad." I slid my fingers into his hair and leaned down, kissing the side of his face.

He lifted up and pulled me down into a long kiss before standing up and pulling me toward the bed. "Fuck, you taste good. Where do you want me, baby?"

"Everywhere." I pulled at his shirt and helped him out of his jeans. He pulled off his boxer briefs, and I froze in place. Fuck me he was big. Too big. There was no way. Not for my first time.

"Touch me," he commanded and reached for my hands. He wrapped both of them around his erection and stroked himself, thrusting a little as he locked eyes with me. "Talk to me. I want to hear what you think. What you feel."

"I'm so lost right now." I pulled at the tip of his dick, wetting my fingers with his precum. "I feel a million things, but most of all, I just want to taste you."

"Good. Do it." He pressed my shoulders, and I sat down on the edge of the bed in my jeans and shoes, but nothing else. "Put your mouth on me. Suck hard and take as much as you can."

I nodded and gripped his cock again, stroking him from tip to base. I leaned over and wrapped my lips around his thick head, tonguing the little opening at the end. Salty lust filled my mouth, and the moan that left me had him pressing forward. He had my hair down, and his fingers wound around a thick chunk of it in no time.

"God, yes. Please don't stop, Bailey. Suck until I come, baby." He held my hair tightly and pressed his cock deeper into my mouth. I gripped his thigh with my free hand and pumped the other hand up and down his shaft. My fingers didn't come close to touching, which excited and scared the shit out of me.

His moans mixed with the sound of me sucking hard and fast filled the room. My body ached for attention, my pussy wet and contracting like he was already inside of me, my nipples so hard they hurt.

"That's it, Angel. So close." He reached down and gripped one of my breasts softly, kneading it. "Ever been titty-fucked, Bailey?"

I mumbled no and groaned again as I neared an orgasm. His words mixed with the delicious taste of him filling up my mouth were almost enough.

"I'm going to touch every part of you." He gripped my hair and stilled me as he lifted his chin to the air. "Drink it. Now. Drink all of it."

"Mmmmhmmm." I leaned in and took every ounce of come he gave me, licking at his shaft and sucking hard at the tip of his dick. "So delicious," I mumbled and moved down to tongue his balls.

"Fuck!" He moved back and pressed his hands to his knees. "Fuck, fuck, fuck. That was so damn good, baby."

"Yeah, it was." I pressed my hands to my knees and took a shaky breath. "Jer. I-"

"Jeremy? Are you still here?" His mother's voice resounded just outside the bedroom door.

"Yeah. I'll be out shortly, Mom. Austin is with Nina."

"Are you in there alone?" She sounded put-off, but then again, she always did to me.

I stood up and covered my breasts with my arms. He lifted his hand to calm me and moved behind me, wrapping me in a tight hug.

"Yep. Be out in a bit. Go back to bed." He licked up the side of my neck and slipped his hand into the front of my jeans and down into my panties. His thick fingers pressed down between my bare lips into the sticky hot wetness pooling at my entrance. He groaned and pressed his mouth to the side of my neck. "I need to fuck you so bad. You have no idea how badly I needed to find you this wet."

I bit my tongue and tried to pull from him, but he wasn't letting me go anywhere. "Jer-"

"No." He kissed my ear. "Come for me."

"No." I pulled away again, but he held on tight and rimmed my pussy, dipping his middle finger into me.

I bucked against him.

His mother's voice rose. "Where is Bailey?"

"No clue, Mom. Be out soon. Rhys and Ellen are in the den. Check on her in there, but leave me be." He bit down on the side of my shoulder and pressed his finger deep inside my slit, fucking me hard and fast as I moved against him and tried not to scream. I was on the edge, dangling over by a string.

"Fine!" His mother didn't sound to happy, but at least she was leaving from in front of the fucking door.

"Come. Now." He pressed his mouth against my ear. "I know you need to. I can feel it all over you. Wet my fingers and next my tongue, and the next time... my dick."

I cried out and gripped his wrist as I jerked against him, fucking myself against his palm as heat burst through the center of my stomach.

He had me on my back, my jeans down and his mouth pressed to my wet center before I could protest. He drank me down before sliding his fingers back into me again and forcing me over the edge three more times.

I glanced down to find his mouth spread open as he sucked on my sensitive bud and his eyes locked on me.

I knew what he wanted, and I had no doubt that he would get it.

He wanted me drowning in lust and maybe even love for him.

Too late. I was already there.

JEREMY

"So you had a good holiday?" Mayhem pulled at the hose beside me as we worked to wash one of our three firetrucks.

"Yeah. I really did." I tried to focus on the task at hand, but my thoughts kept racing back to Bailey. To the feeling of her quivering beneath me, to her taste, to the fucking sound of her crying out as she came.

I knew it was much more than lust, but the lusty parts were to damn good. They were healing in ways I couldn't explain if someone asked me to.

"Who was the girl?" He popped me in the arm, bringing me back from my reverie.

"She was my best friend's little sister." I shrugged and reached up to work on one of the windows.

"She was damn fine. Are you-"

"Yeah," I barked and glanced down at the big bastard. "I am."

"Well. That's great news, man." He smiled up at me. "We were all hoping that maybe you were dating again."

I chuckled, releasing the stress from my shoulders as I relaxed. I just knew he was going to ask about taking her out or say something about getting into her panties. Neither comment would have been okay.

"I've been dating for about eighteen months." I gave him a look.

"Yeah, but that shit with your mom doesn't count."

"Watch it," I warned him. "You know Mom is just trying to help."

"Yeah. I get it, but it looks like you don't need any help." He moved back. "I'm heading out. This fucker is almost done."

"Enjoy your night." I glanced back and smiled as Bailey stood next to the open door, leaning against the door frame. "Damn. You look good. Real good." I got off the truck and jogged toward her. "Where you been the last few days?"

"Work." She wrapped her arms around my neck, and the world felt right.

I leaned down and kissed her a few times as I drew her deeper into my arms. "Let's go to my office."

"What? No." She pulled back a little, but I didn't let her go too far. Her perky breasts felt too good on my chest to give too much leeway.

"Why not? No one will come in there."

She glanced around and back up at me. "Not right now. Maybe soon."

There was something she wasn't telling me, but we were spending the next evening together at her place. I figured I could push her a little more then.

"Alright. Tell me what you're doing here?" I leaned down and kissed her one more time before the sound of the guy's having fun with it had me moving back. "Fuck off. Get busy or run laps," I barked.

She laughed and pulled at my arm. "Come outside with me for a few minutes."

"Yeah, sure." I wrapped my arm around her shoulders and pulled her to my side as we made our way out in front of the fire station. "You get Rhys back to the airport okay?"

"He's already halfway home I bet." She turned to face me and pressed her hands to my chest. "I need to talk to you about tomorrow night."

"Hey. If you aren't ready for me to spend the night, no worries. I know this is moving fast." I reached up and touched the side of her face before scowling. "Why is your hair up? It needs to be down so I can touch it."

She gave me a look, growled and pulled it down. "Better?"

"God, yes." I slipped both hands into it and leaned down to consume her mouth. Everything made sense with her pressed against me. All of my worries over Austin or my pain of Laila disappeared for a few minutes. It was more than I ever could have hoped for.

She lifted up, pressing into the kiss until I slid my hands down and cupped her fine ass.

"Jer." She moved back and popped me in the chest softly.

"What? Shit. You're turning me on, woman. I'm about to turn caveman and throw you over my shoulder and take you to the office for a spanking."

"Don't even think about it." Her sweet mouth turned up in a quirky smile.

"Shit. That's all I think about." I reached out and pulled her back against me. "Talk to me. What do you wanna say, Angel? I'm listening."

"I was thinking about your mom." She rubbed her hands over my chest and up to my neck as she studied me. I wanted to flirt some more, but I could tell she was headed somewhere serious.

"What about her?" I reached up and tucked a few strands of hair behind her ear before sliding my fingers through her silky locks. "She say something to you?"

"No." She glanced down.

"Liar."

Her laugh was sweet. Soft. More than enough to leave me rock hard and thinking about one thing. Owning her.

"No, really." Bailey glanced up, and the worry in her eyes was more than apparent. "She just wants the best for you, you know?"

"I'm a thirty-two year old man with a son. I'm pretty sure the best for me is what I say it is." I cupped her face and forced her to look at me. "I want to try this thing out with you, baby. I think it can go somewhere really fast and really strong. Don't you?"

"I don't know." She pulled back and took a shaky breath. "What if I'm not the right person to bring into Austin's life?"

"Where is this coming from? We just decided to try each other out on Thursday and it's Sunday. You've talked yourself out of us over a weekend?" Worry flooded me. Damn. Could I stand letting her in only to have her walk away? No. Not a fucking chance.

"I don't know." She turned and gripped her own hair as she let out a soft growl. "I'm just worried that I'm not enough."

"That's bullshit, Bailey." I moved up behind her, wrapping my arms around her and squeezing her breast softly as I leaned down and kissed her ear a few times. "Stop fucking this up. It just started. How long have you wanted me?"

"Forever."

"Right. So why you pushing me away already? Am I not enough for you? Am I not the guy you thought I would be."

She whipped around with anger on her face. "No. Never. Don't even say that."

"Then you stop acting it." I gripped her hips and stepped up, leaning down and kissing the hell out of her. I pressed my tongue deep into her sweet mouth and coaxed hers back into my mouth before sucking and licking at it.

She whimpered and gripped my shirt tightly. The pretty little thing had worked up a situation in her head that didn't exist. I wasn't going to go three or four days without seeing her again. She was young, and so was the relationship. We had to figure out a groove, and she had to gain her confidence in me. She had to see what I saw, feel what I felt.

"Hey," I whispered against her soft, wet lips. "Don't think about this shit again. Promise me. Now."

She nodded. "Okay. I'm just scared."

"Don't be. Whether anything becomes of us, I'm one of the good guys. I'll always be waiting just behind Rhys to catch you. You get that right?"

Tears blurred her eyes. "I think so."

"Good. We'll talk some more tomorrow night. Let's make dinner together and then make love. I want to feel every part of you, baby." I leaned down and kissed her again, stealing her breath from her mouth and leaving her wobbly on her feet. It's the way I always wanted her to feel when she was with me.

"What about Laila?" she blurted out as her face paled.

"What about her?" I reached out and cupped Bailey's face. "She's gone and I have to move on."

"Can you do that?" She wrapped her slender fingers around my wrist.

"I don't know." I glanced up at the sky. My turn to take a shaky breath. I let it out slowly and tilted my chin down until the most beautiful innocent eyes stared up at me. "I think I can, but I'm going to need your help."

"I want to help you in any way I can." Her voice softened as her eyes widened a little.

"Then make love to me tomorrow night. Help me wash away the memories I keep holding onto." I leaned down and brushed my nose by hers as my eyes closed. "I want to fall so deep in love with you that I have to look at pictures to remember the pain."

"I want that too," she whispered against my lips. "Tomorrow night."

I opened my eyes and smiled. "Behave at work and get off early tomorrow. I'll be there no later than four. Good?"

"Very good." She stood there for a few seconds, just watching me. She might have wanted me in her life more than anyone else had, but I needed her in mine. I trusted her with my heart, which was a weird place to be. But history with someone did that shit. It opened people up to possibility.

Even the most jaded lives.

Lives like mine.

Guys like me.

BAILEY

"You're late." I smiled as I opened the door and moved back. Jeremy's dark hair was wet from a shower from what I gathered, and he smelled like soap and aftershave. I breathed in deeply and reached for the flowers he handed me.

"No, I'm early." He handed off the roses and reached for me, pulling me against his strong chest. "And you're gorgeous. Did you know I thought about you all day today?"

"You did not." I lifted up on my toes and pressed my lips to his as I cupped his face.

"I did." He kissed me again, his lips so soft and wet, his aggression to get the night moving more than obvious.

I licked at his mouth and moved back, turning and walking into the kitchen. "I made a homemade lasagna. Do you like Italian?"

"I'm warm-blooded and big. I love anything that a woman cooks for me." He moved up behind me and wrapped his arms around me. "Let me have you for an appetizer, then we can eat."

"What?" I squeaked.

"You heard me." He forced me to turn toward him. "Why are you so shy around me?"

"I haven't been with too many guys, Jer." I gripped his large shoulders as he lifted me and set me on the counter next to the stove.

"Good. I like that." He leaned in for a long kiss as he ran his hands down my legs and gripped my ankles. "Feet on the counter. Lean back."

"You just got here." I gripped the edge of the counter and leaned back.

"Yeah, and I'm going to start off the night by eating my pussy." He pulled my long skirt up over my thighs and licked his lips as he glanced up at me. "I love that you shave yourself."

Warmth filled my chest and coated my cheeks. "You're too much."

"No, baby. I'm not nearly enough." He moved to his knees and leaned in, breathing in deeply as he slipped the back of his fingers under my silky blue panties. The backs of his fingers were rough, but in a good way. "I've been waiting for this night since Thanksgiving."

"Be easy with me," I whispered as he leaned in and licked around my panties until his tongue slipped under them.

"Never. It's not happening." He tugged my panties aside and flicked his tongue over my soft flesh. "You're already wet, bad girl. You were thinking about me."

"Mmhmm," I closed my eyes and let out a contented sigh as he sucked at one of my lips while he pressed a finger deep into my slit. "I always think about you."

He leaned back and brushed his thumb over my clit as he pressed another finger into me. "You're so tight, Bailey."

"I only use one finger," I mumbled and arched my back as my body began to purr.

"Open your eyes and look at me," he commanded.

I didn't hesitate. "I need you inside of me."

"I am inside of you, Angel. You want something else? Tell me." He leaned in and licked at my pussy again as he continued to watch me. Never in my life had I seen something so fucking sexy.

"I want your cock in me." I reached down and ran my fingers through his hair. "I want you to be my first."

He lifted an eyebrow and moved back, but continued his slow

assault on my pussy. Thick fingers pumping in and out of me in a slow rhythm while he played with the bundle of nerves at the top of my mound.

"Your first? You haven't slept with anyone?" His eyes darkened just a little.

I moaned loudly and pressed down on his fingers. "No. I'm a little nervous, but I trust you."

"I would never hurt you." He leaned back down and sucked my clit back into his mouth. His tongue danced around, teasing me toward the edge of orgasm. The sound of my body sucking wildly at his fingers had me bucking against him as my orgasm tore me apart.

He continued his assault, standing and leaning over as he pumped his fingers deeper into my convulsing channel. Warmth and pleasure mixed with lust as I gripped the counter and cried out over and over.

"Stop, baby. Enough." I pushed at his shoulder.

He pulled his fingers from me and smiled. "Not even close." He moved down, pressing his mouth around my opening and tonguing me as he licked and sucked every drop of my orgasm down.

I came again just watching him.

"Such a good girl." He stood up and locked eyes with me as he patted my pussy softly over and over. "You know I plan on fucking you a few times tonight, right, Bailey?"

I nodded. "Yeah. I want you to."

"I know you do, Angel. Let's go to the bedroom."

"What about dinner?" I sat up and took his hand, sliding off the counter with his help.

"We'll eat in a little while." He turned off the oven and took my hand before leading me to the back room.

"We need condoms, Jeremy."

He patted his back pocket. "I got us covered. I hate the damn things, but until you get on the pill, they're necessary. My shit's potent. We fuck without them and you're going to be giving me the best gift a man can get. A baby." He turned to face me as we moved into the darkness of my bedroom.

A rush of fear moved through me. What if I jacked things up?

What if my inexperience made me look ridiculous? What if I didn't feel good to him?

"Hey. Stop thinking and get over here." He smiled and ran his hands down the side of my hair to cup my face again. "No more thinking. I want you to memorize every good moment from our first time together."

"From my first time in general." I leaned against him and closed my eyes as he moved down to kiss me. The musky taste of my come on his lips was odd at first, but the more I let myself go, the more I enjoyed it. Enjoyed him. Enjoyed the freedom to simply be a woman who was wanted so fucking bad by a man.

"That's it." He licked at my lips and moved back to pull my shirt over my head before slipping my skirt down and pulling my panties with it. He stood and turned me around, removing my bra and taking the time to massage my breasts before tugging at my nipples. "You just relax tonight and feel me, hm?"

"Okay," I whispered and crawled up on my bed as he popped my ass and moved back to take off his clothes.

I laid down on my back and watched him as he undressed slowly for me. He had to be the most beautiful thing I'd ever seen in my life.

"You look so beautiful like that. I want to see you laid out on a bed for me every day." He leaned over and pulled a condom from his jeans, but didn't put it on. He tossed it up on the bed bedside me and crawled onto the bottom. His muscles were flexed like he'd just come from the gym, and his cock was thick, hard and standing at full attention. "I like to fuck a lot. Maybe I should have warned you." He leaned down and brushed his lips over the inside of my calf.

I moaned and gripped the sheets. "I'm good with you wanting to do anything you want to. I just want to be beneath you when you do it."

He chuckled deep in his chest. "Beneath me. Above me. In front of me." He nipped at my inner thigh. "I love deeply, Bailey, but I lust even deeper."

"God," I moaned as he kissed my pussy before moving up. "I don't deserve you."

"Bullshit." He pressed his knees into the bed and gripped his cock as he sat back on his heels between my legs. "I'm going to deflower you bareback, baby. I want to feel you release yourself to me, okay?"

"Isn't it bloody?" I cringed at the thought.

"Yeah, but it's okay. Just relax and enjoy the fact that you and I are about to become one." He ran his hand up my stomach and between my breasts as he gripped his thick cock and positioned it against my entrance.

I moaned loudly and gripped his hand as nerves and excitement dance in my stomach. "I've wanted this for as long as I could remember."

"Good. It's yours, baby girl." He pressed in a little and gripped the base of my neck loosely. "Relax. Let me in. You're fighting me. Just think about how good this big dick is going to feel tucked deep inside your tight little needy slit."

"Fuck," I arched my back and spread my legs farther and he pressed down on my chest and forced a few more inches inside of me. It felt as if I were going to burst, but the pain of stretching around him moved into pleasure as he released his cock and pressed his thumb to my clit. The slow circles he made around my sensitive nerves were enough to have me dripping with wetness.

"There you go. She wants me deeper, Bailey. You good with that, Angel?" He glanced up and locked eyes with me.

Love.

All I saw was love in his eyes. My emotions went on high alerts as tears filled my eyes. I needed to know that he cared about me, that he saw us going much farther than a night together.

He pulled back a little. "Am I hurting you, baby? You gotta talk to me."

"No." I reached for him and pulled him down on top of me. His strong, thick chest pressed against mine, and he kissed me softly.

"What's going on?" He rolled his hips, pulling out and pressing back in a little.

I wrapped my legs around him and let out a breath I didn't realize I was holding. "I'm just scared."

"Of what?" He reached down and lifted my leg a little as he pushed in farther.

I cried out in pain. "You not wanting me after tonight."

He smiled. "I want you for a lot of nights after this. Every night until you kick my ass out." He pressed his elbows beside my face and wiped my tears away. "Focus on me while I get past your tightness. I'm going to push in cause you're ready, but I need you to breath out and think about the delicious fucks were going to have after this moment. I'm going to take you places you never dreamed possible. Highs you didn't even know existed."

"I want that. For me and you." I pulled him down and kissed him hard as he thrust, breaking my cherry and lodging his huge cock balls deep inside of me.

"Fuck," he groaned and lifted up as he rolled his hips. "I'm in. I need the condom."

I reached for it as the burn of pain faded.

He pulled out, slipped the condom on and moved back on top of me. "Hold me while I lose myself in you."

I wrapped my arms around him and kissed his neck, chest and mouth while he took his time working me over the edge several times before joining me.

No matter what happened from there on out, some part of me would always belong to him.

Scary enough, it wasn't just my virginity.

It was my heart.

17

JEREMY

A few days after making love to my girl, I sat in my office, staring at the picture of Laila and Austin. I wanted to get her blessing on Bailey, but it was stupid. She'd have given it no doubt, but me wanting it felt silly or contrite. I put the picture in a drawer of my desk, though it hurt to do it.

I had to start moving on. Bailey was partially the key to that, but the majority of the strength had to come from somewhere inside of me. It had felt impossible up to that point, but holding Bailey in my arms all night earlier in the week and hearing her whisper my name in the dark pushed me toward healing.

To be loved again. To be needed. It's all I wanted, but it had to be the right woman, and thankfully I felt like I'd found her.

The fire alarm at the station caused me to jump to my feet as it pulled me from my thoughts. My heart raced as I jogged toward the pole and started to yell out orders. As the Captain, I shouldn't have been going anywhere near the flames, but we were still short staffed as most of the guys were volunteers at the station anyway.

"Fuck," I growled as I realized we were going in one short.

"It's going to be alright, Cap." Mayhem jogged past me and started to shout out orders to the guys.

I nodded and pursed my lips. Every inch of me wanted to take command, to make my orders the ones that were heard, but once again, I moved into second place. We'd be fully staffed soon, and having the guys not pay attention to Mayhem would be... well, mayhem.

I smirked at the joke and got dressed with efficiency. We were all in the truck and headed to the fire within minutes.

"Update," I barked and sat down.

"Structure fire, Cap." Mayhem gripped his hands together and glanced down.

Something was wrong. "Keep going, John."

He glanced up with a bit of terror in his eyes as I called him by his real name. "It's collapsing, and several people have perished, Sir. Two kids and three adults."

I nodded and held his stare. "We're going to get the rest out. Be smart. Be safe."

He swallowed and stood back up before barking orders at everyone like he was pissed at the whole crew. He was scared. We all were when lives were at stake. It was fine to fight a fire and only have to worry about our own lives, but to have to worry about people in the burning building was a whole new level of fear.

We pulled up and the guys hustled off. I jogged down the stairs right behind them and moved over to the hydrant.

"Hose!" I yelled and got down on my knees. Memories flooded me as I knelt there waiting. The blaze before me warmed my face and forced me to look up.

My life had been a mosaic of broken moments, but maybe everyone's was. From losing part of my sight on vacation in the Air Force to being given medical leave and having to walk away from my dream to losing Laila.

The guys pulled the hose my way, and I moved quickly as I let myself move through the pinpoints of pain and joy.

My acceptance into the Air Force and Rhys right beside me. Happy as fuck.

My wedding day.

Austin being born.

Thanksgiving. The resurrection of hope to a broken soul. My soul.

"Done." I bolted up and raced toward the front of the group standing around. "Back up. All the way across the street. Now!" I moved civilians back and helped several with their stuff as the guys started fighting the fire.

"My son! Please! He's in there!!" A woman grabbed the front of my uniform, crying and screaming.

"Where. Point to where." I turned toward the building.

"Up there. Fifth floor. I thought he was behind us, but he must have gone back for something."

"How old is he?" I moved toward the building as she called after me.

"He's eight!"

"We got a little boy. Eight years old up that way on floor five. I'm going in." I pulled my mask down and grabbed a few things. Mayhem moved up next to me and nodded, acknowledging that he would follow my lead.

We moved into the building and carefully made our way to the fifth floor as fire licked at us from all sides. Sweat dripped down my face and clouded my vision a little. The dark smoke rolling off the burning building made it hard as hell to see anything.

Mayhem tapped my shoulder and moved past me before getting down on the ground. He was going into the apartment to check for the child.

I nodded and squatted down. Turning in a full circle, a cold chill ran down my back. Something was off. I could feel it with every cell in my body.

Moving toward the apartment behind me, I crawled half on my belly while trying to hold the damn equipment I had with me. I knew better than to bring anything that I had to carry, and yet... I'd done just that.

"Help!" The sound of a little scream caused me to move faster. Why the hell was the kid in another apartment?

A moment later, I spotted him in the corner of the kitchen in the apartment across the hall from the one his mother mentioned. He was curled up with a little puppy yapping and trying to get out of his arms.

"Hey, buddy." I pulled up my mask and gave him a warm smile. "We were looking for you."

"Miss Terry's puppy was crying behind the door. I heard him so-"

"Let's get you out of here, and you can explain." I reached out and pulled him into my arms. "Hold onto the puppy tightly, okay?"

"Yes, Sir." He buried his face against my chest and started to cry.

I hustled him out of the building, running as fast as I could. The little guy was going to have to go to the hospital because of smoke inhalation, but he would be safe.

"Oh, God. Thank you so much." His mother ran toward us, taking him out of my arms. He was small for eight, but it was a good thing for the situation.

I pulled my helmet off and smiled down at him. "You were brave, but if you're ever in this situation again, you need to get out of the building, okay?"

"Thank you again." The mom gripped my arm and gave me a teary smile.

"No problem." I turned and jogged back toward the building. "Where is Mayhem?" I glanced around.

"I don't know." One of the younger guys pulled his mask off and started to yell for John.

"Fuck." I moved around and realized that he wasn't there. "I'm going back in."

I made my way back into the building, the heat almost unbearable. The sound of the structure falling around me only caused me to move faster. I made it to the fifth floor and pulled my mask up.

"John! Where are you, buddy?" I moved toward the apartment he originally went into while trying to watch my step.

"Here. I'm in here, Cap!"

I moved carefully into the room to see his leg stuck in the floor. He was yanking at it with what looked like all of his might.

"Dammit." I raced over and knelt down to pull at the board around him. One cracked, and he fell back and landed on his ass. "No.

Let's go. No time for resting. This fucker is about to collapse around us."

"I'm behind you." He got up and moved toward the door.

I pushed at his back, making him go first. "Stick to the edges. Go."

We moved forward until we were back out in the grass. He surprised me by turning around and picking me up in a big bear hug.

"You saved my life." He squeezed me tightly and laughed.

"Get busy putting this fire out," I barked and patted his chest. "Thank me later with a beer."

"Fuck yes." He moved toward the fire with the other guys, hoses in hand to take the beast down.

Gratefulness swam through me, and two people came to mind that I wanted to see.

My little guy, and my girl.

"What? Now?" Bailey stood at the open door of her apartment in PJ pants and a tank top. No bra, and hopefully no panties. Her nipples were budded and poking at the material. It took every ounce of reserve not to take her tits in my hands and play with them.

"Yes, now." I smiled and walked into the apartment.

She turned to face me in time for me to pull her firmly against me. I kissed her with a passion I almost had forgotten I had pent up inside of me.

I licked at her perfect lips before kissing the tip of her nose. "Go put on something warm. We're going on a date. I've had a horrible couple of days. No arguing. Get to it, or you *won't* get a spanking."

She laughed and pulled me down for another series of kisses, speaking between each one. "I. Don't. Like. Spankings."

"Then you haven't had the right man give you one." I gripped her sweet face and kissed her one more time. "Go. Now. I have plans for you later, and you're eating into them."

"Does your plans include you eating into something?" She laughed as I growled low in my chest.

I popped her perfect ass as she walked toward the bedroom. "Can't we just cuddle on the couch and watch a movie."

"Nope. Not right now." I walked into the kitchen and made my way to the fridge. After downing a beer, I walked back into the kitchen to wait for her.

She walked down the hall in a pair of tight jeans, a pretty white sweater, and some knee-high boots. She looked like a fucking model. She was working to get her hair up into a ponytail, but I gave her a look.

"Not a chance. Your hair stays down around me. You know this." I reached out as she flung the rubber band across the room and sighed.

"It's unruly in the wind." Her fingers pressed into my chest as she glanced up at me.

Marry me. I stiffened at the words running through my head in a loop. I'd know her all of my life, and yet I didn't really know her. I trusted her and her family, and Rhys was my closest friend and always would be, but I didn't know her dreams and fears.

That's what today is about.

"You're so beautiful." I reached up and slid my fingers into her hair, massaging her scalp as I studied her features. My cock woke up, and my heart started to beat faster as I stood there with her in my arms.

"You think so?" She gave me a quirky smile. "Where are you taking me that's so damn important?"

"To a really late lunch in the park, then the museum and then ice skating." I leaned down and kissed her softly. "Then we're coming home to my house. I'm going to bath you and take my time memorizing every wicked curve of your body. Then I'm going to teach you how numbers work in the bed, then-"

"Numbers in the bed?" She chuckled. "What are you talking about? It's official. Your dick is talking for you now."

I laughed and gripped her hand. After sliding it down my erection through my jeans, I nipped at her lips. "Sixty-nine tonight, sweet girl. I wanna hear you cry out around my cock when you come for me."

She shivered, and I loved it. The effect I had on her was an aphrodisiac.

"That's so hot," she whispered and slid her fingers into my hair before pulling me down for a probing kiss. I indulged and gripped her tight ass, squeezing as she undulated her hips forward. She was horny, and I wasn't far behind her.

"Date first." I kissed her again and turned to grab her coat. "Put this on. It's fucking freezing out there."

"I'm turned on. I want to stay here." She wrapped her arms around me from behind and squeezed tightly.

"You wet?" I pressed my hand to the door as she groaned lustily.

"Very."

I turned and smiled before walking to the couch and dropped down. "Come here and let me take care of you. Then we'll go."

"Take care of me?" She walked over with a naughty smile on her lips.

"Hell yeah. Turn around and sit on my lap, baby." I reached for her, turning her around and pulling her into my lap.

"Pants on?" She turned her head and glanced up at me.

"Mhmm." I gripped her chin and kissed her softly as I slid my free hand into her pants and panties. The little minx was sloppy wet, her pussy so warm and inviting. I slid my fingers past her clit and pressed the middle one into her tight hole as she moaned and closed her eyes.

It didn't take more than a few minutes of driving my finger deep inside her slit and pressing my palm firmly over her clit to have her writhing on my lap. My cock was thick and hard, but I wanted to wait. Not everything had to be about sex. She needed to know that I wanted so much more than that.

"God, Jeremy. I'm going to-"

"Good," I cut her off and kissed her harder as I picked up my pace. "Come for me."

She screamed and thrashed against me, her ass rubbing over my erection fast and hard.

I closed my eyes as my balls contracted and came with her.

We were both panting as I patted her pussy softly and kissed her lips. "Such a good girl. You're so beautiful when you let yourself go and enjoy your body."

"Only then?" She smiled and kissed me before pulling my hand from her panties and heading to the bathroom. "Let's go. I'm excited to go on our first date."

"Sex before our first date, hmm... either you're a slut, or I am." I stood up and smiled.

"Definitely you," she called from down the hallway with a laugh quick to follow.

I nodded. She was totally right, but it was all good. I had a beautiful woman to be a *slut* with now. All was well with the world.

18

BAILEY

"It's freezing out there." I gripped Jeremy's hand through our gloves and snuggled closer to him. "Let's just get a sandwich and soup at that cute little bistro over there. There's no way I'm eating in the park."

"Where is your sense of adventure?" He smiled down at me, setting the butterflies in my stomach dancing around. How in the world a handsome man like him could like a simple girl like me was a mystery, but I wasn't going to fight it. I couldn't. I'd wanted him too long.

"In the bedroom," I replied very matter of factly.

He laughed and released my hand to pull me closer. "You're too sexy for your own good, Angel."

"Yeah?" I wrapped my arm around his lower back and snuggled against him. "When do I get to see Austin again, Jer?"

"Soon." He smiled down at me. "I'll set something up. I want to take it slow with him. I haven't dated since Laila died."

"So, he doesn't know about all the blind dates your mom sends you on? I mean, you haven't had any of them make it past the date phase so that they meet your family?"

"Hell, no. Have you seen the women my mother sets me up with?" He laughed and leaned over to kiss the side of my head as we walked up the bistro. He released me and opened the door. "Let me tell you some of these stories over lunch."

I laughed. "I'd love that."

"I bet you would." He popped my butt playfully and moved up behind me in line. "Bad girl."

"Only for you," I mumbled and wrapped my arms around his arms as he held me tightly from behind. The warmth of being in his arms was everything I thought it would be and then some. The sound of his mother's voice filled my head, and I thought about telling him about my brief conversation with her.

She didn't like me. I didn't have to analyze it. She'd been really blunt at Thanksgiving.

"Bailey, right?" His mother gave me the once over as she tilted her head to the side. The look on her face was less than pleasant, almost like she'd eaten a lemon.

"Yes, ma'am." I forced a smile.

"I don't know what you're doing here, but I hope it's just because you're Rhys's little sister and you needed a place to be for the holidays." She pursed her lips as her eyes darkened.

"Um... Yes?" She'd caught me off-guard. I'd always been more than good enough for my own family, but it was odd standing there feeling like less than for Jeremy's mother.

"You do realize that Jeremy isn't interested in anyone under the age of thirty, right? He's looking for a mother for Austin, not a part-time girlfriend to fix his male yearnings."

"Of course." I reached up and brushed my hand over the top of my head. "I'm just a friend."

"Good. Keep it that way." She turned and busied herself with the kitchen as I stood there in mild shock. It took me a second to get my legs working so I could get the fuck out of the kitchen and away from her.

"Miss?" The guy at the counter smiled. "You ready to order?"

"Baby?" Jeremy leaned around and smiled at me. "You okay?"

"Oh yeah. I'm good." I moved up and ordered before pulling out my check card.

"Not a chance." Jeremy pushed my hand away as I went to give the guy my card. "You don't pay when I'm here. Did your parents not raise you right, girl?"

I smiled and rolled my eyes before walking over and finding a booth. I sat down and let out a short sigh. Jeremy's mother did *not* approve of me, though I'd done nothing to deserve it. I couldn't help that I was six years younger than him, which didn't seem like that big of an age gap the more I thought about it.

"Hey. What's up with you?" He handed me a drink and moved to the other side of the booth. "You went from being here with me to lost in your head. Talk to me."

"No. I'm good." I took the cup and took a small sip. "Tell me about your family, Jer. I know you have Nina and your mother, but where's your dad? Rhys and I never really talked about your personal life or anything. I want to know about you."

"Yeah, sure." He glanced down at his drink and smiled. "My dad was everything. So fun and full of life. My mom is a bit of a rich sour-puss at times, but my dad was all fun and games."

"But your dad was the only one that made all the money in your family, right? I remember Rhys telling me that your mom stayed home." I smiled as Jeremy looked up. His warm brown eyes drew me in deep, and I wanted to move to the other side of the table. "He was jealous. You know both of our parents worked all the time, so we had to fend for ourselves."

"I was lucky that Dad made it in business." He nodded. "Mom stayed home and kept the house and watched after us, but she came from big money. Her family owns billions of dollars of real estate in Europe and Greece."

"Oh. That makes sense." I sat back as the server delivered our sandwich/soup combos. "So your dad grew up wealthy too?"

"No." Jeremy picked up his spoon and smiled at me. "You praying or am I?"

"Um. You." I bowed my head, a little surprised by his desire to pray. Was he religious?

He went through a short, but beautiful blessing. The sound of his deep voice talking to God was a little much for me. It pushed my desire to know him more, to be loved by him, to belong to him a little farther along.

"So my dad was a scrapper," he started. "Born in the lower middle class and had to earn everything he got. He was smart as hell and figured out how to create a business selling a specialized pipe to water companies." He shrugged. "When he died, he'd amassed a few billion dollars in wealth through various properties, his company, and investments."

"Oh. Wow." I leaned over and blew on my soup. "I had no idea it was to that level."

"Yeah, but I told my mom and Nina that I don't want any of that money."

"Why not?" I took a small bite of my soup and watched him. Money was the least of my concerns. It was in abundance everywhere, but it took a toll on those who went after it with fervor. I wasn't interested in paying the price it demanded. So I lived my simple life, as did my parents.

"I don't know. Maybe one day if my wife wants to have some of the finer things in life, I'll consider taking my inheritance, but I don't need it right now, and I don't want Austin growing up like mom did." He locked eyes with me. For a moment it felt like he was inviting me into that future.

I love you sat on the tip of my tongue.

"I see." I glanced down at my soup. "Your mother is trying to find you a wife then? I mean, with all of these random dates and stuff."

He chuckled. "Yes, but I won't be going on anymore, obviously. I have you." He reached across the table and squeezed my hand. "I had a really big fire today that I had to put out. There were several times that I had to run back into the building to save someone, and I couldn't get you off my mind."

"Cause I'm hot?" I crinkled my nose as he laughed.

112

"Oh, Lord. You are fucking hot, but we're going to have to work on your humor."

"Hey!" I smiled and pulled my hand back as he released it. "Thank you though. For telling me that."

"Tell me about the paint brushes I saw in the living room while I was making love to you a little while ago." He licked the side of his mouth as his eyes darkened just a little.

A lusty shiver raced through me. "Really? You're going to turn me on in a sandwich shop?"

"Baby, I'm going to work at turning you on in every place we go together." He lifted both of his eyebrows. "There's a small bathroom in the back if you need some help with-"

"I'm good!" My cheeks burned with embarrassment as I gave a nervous laugh and picked up my sandwich. "I love painting, but I suck at it." I shrugged. "It's been a hobby since I was little. My mom painted."

"Nice. I want to see some of your stuff, Bailey."

"No way." I shook my head and took a big bite of my sandwich.

"Hey." His expression softened. "I want in, okay? Not just into your body or your heart." He reached back over and intertwined his fingers with mine. "I want into your life."

My heart swelled in my chest, and it suddenly seemed so damn hard to get enough air into my lungs.

"Okay," I whispered and took another bite of my sandwich. We stared at each other, making small talk as we finished the meal. I had no doubt at all that *this* was what love felt like.

It was pure and sweet, sexy and wicked. It left me breathless and scared as hell to take another step forward.

"You ready to check out the art museum?" He wrapped an arm around my shoulders as we walked toward the gallery. Snow started to fall from above us in large flakes as we moved out onto the sidewalk.

I paused and lifted my face as I closed my eyes. "Yes, I'm ready. Just a sec."

He laughed. "So... wait or go?"

"Wait, then go?" I breathed in deeply. "I love the snow so much. It's refreshing."

Strong arms wrapped around me tightly. "So is being with you. I never thought I could move on from Laila, but there's a spark of hope inside of me."

"You loved her deeply, didn't you?" I put my hands on his forearms and locked gazes with him.

"I did. The day she died, everything changed. I kept thinking that the only way to set it right would be to die beside her." His expression tightened, and the pain on his face caused tears to blur my vision. "But I had Austin, you know?"

"Yeah. I'm glad you did." I moved farther into his arms and kissed his chin as he continued.

"I was a bastard though. I went into every blazing building I could in hopes of finding her ghost there, or maybe letting an accident take me out of my misery. As much as I wanted to live for Aus, it got harder and harder the lonelier life got." He reached down and brushed my tears away as they started to drop. "And then Mom with her stupid dating shit."

I smiled as he snorted and chuckled. "She was only trying to help."

"I know, and I went with it because of that, but no one was like Laila. That deep burning desire that used to live inside of me to get home to her, to hold her, to just be around her. It seemed like that feeling only belonged to *her,* which leaves me where now that she's gone?"

I reached up and cupped the side of his face. "I want to make it better for you."

He smiled and kissed my palm. "That was how I felt up until about a month ago."

More tears for me. "And then?" I squeaked out.

"Then I walked into a shit-hole of a restaurant in search of the date from hell, and this sexy little bartender was there. Damn, she was fine."

I laughed and pulled my hands down to rest on his chest. "It's all about that ass, hm?"

"It started that way." He brushed his nose by mine. "But then I realized who you were, and everything changed. I could trust you from the start. I know your heart. It takes so many factors out of the way, you know?"

"Don't make me fall deeper in love with you, Jer. I've wanted you all my life." I trembled against him as the wind picked up. "If this doesn't work, the fall is already too far for me."

"Nothing is going to stop this thing between us but me and you." He kissed me a few times. "And I'm willing to go all in."

I pressed my lips to his as someone honked beside us.

"Hey! Fancy meeting you here!" Ellen's voice filled up the space around us. "Get in. It's about to start snowing like crazy. I'll drive you crazy kids to wherever you're going."

"Saved by the bell." Jeremy opened the front door and smiled over at me. "Get in, beautiful. Let's finish our date and get back home."

"Or we could just go home?" I wagged my eyebrows and got into the car.

"Not a chance." He closed it behind me and got in the back.

I closed my eyes, and he and Ellen chatted it up on our way over to the Museum. Nothing could stand in the way of our love growing but him or me. Wrong.

His mother could, and something told me that she most certainly would.

JEREMY

TWO WEEKS LATER

"One week until Christmas! Yay!" Austin pounced on the bed and danced around in high excitement.

I laughed and reached down to grab the little tike. "Christmas is for good boys! Santa called and said you were on the *naughty* list!" I rolled over and held myself up as I tickled him good.

"Okay! Daddy! I'm going to pee the bed. Stop!"

"Hands off. No peeing the bed!" I moved off of him and tussled his hair as I shifted to my side of the bed.

He rolled over to face me. "That wasn't the truth. I don't have to pee."

I laughed and pushed him onto his back. "See! That's why you're on the naughty list."

His voice sounded ten years older than he was as he glanced over and gave me a very serious look. "I am not on the naughty list, nor will I ever be, Daddy. I'm always good."

"Good?" I moved back over him and tugged his nightshirt up before blowing on his stomach, making loud fart sounds. "You just lied about having to pee."

"I was kidding." He beat on my back and kicked, barely missing my balls.

I rolled off of him and stood beside the bed. "Kidding? Nope. It's lying."

"I disagree." He got off the bed and stood on the other side of it across from me. "And me and Santa? We're like this..." He lifted his fingers and twisted the first and middle one around each other.

I laughed loudly. "Where do you get this stuff?"

"TV." He smiled and bounded down the hall. "Let's go to the store. One week until Christmas!"

"Yes! Let's do it." I walked over to my dresser and picked up my phone. The picture of me and Bailey at the museum, wrapped around each other was my screen saver. I closed my eyes and let out a painful sigh. "Thank you for another chance. I don't deserve it, but I'm willing to take it."

"Invite Bailey, Daddy!" Austin popped back into my room with his shirt off and one leg in his jeans. He was dragging the other leg behind him.

I laughed and moved over to help him finish getting dressed. "You like Bailey?"

"Oh yeah, but you don't bring her around here much. Why?" He sucked in as I buckled his pants, though they were too big already. "You don't like her as much as I do?"

I smiled. "No. I like her a lot, but I didn't want to bring her over here until I was sure she liked me back."

"Dad." He put his little hands on my chest and gave me a look my mother would be quite proud of. "How could she *not* like you? Everyone likes you."

"This is true." I winked and stood up. "I'll call her and see when she works."

"Okay, but if she works, let's just go eat our lunch with her."

"Okay, Buddy. Go get a shirt and some shoes. Let's get moving."

"You were the one who was still sleeping." He jogged down the hall, leaving me standing there. He was growing up way too fucking fast.

I walked back over and called my girl to see what she was up to. She answered on the first ring, but her voice was filled with sleep.

"Jer?"

"Hi, baby." I paused as my stomach tightened and my cock twitched. Fuck me; she sounded so good. If I hadn't of had Austin with me, I'd have gone over and spent the day in bed with her.

"You okay?" She let out a soft yawn that had my blood pumping hard and fast.

"How do you turn me on with nothing more than three words?" I dropped down on the edge of the bed and grabbed a pillow to hide my hard-on lest the boy come bounding back in.

She giggled. "What are you doing, bad boy? It's early."

"No, it's late according to a three-foot leprechaun that lives in my house." I leaned back and closed my eyes. "We're going shopping for Christmas today. It's a week away."

"Sounds like fun. Just you and Austin?"

"And Nina, and we were hoping you would come too. It's a family tradition of sorts. We go into every store Austin wants to, and he points out what he wants. We write it down and later tonight he makes his Santa list. We started it when Laila passed."

"Of course I'll go. I want to."

"Good. We'll pick you up in an hour. Dress warmly. It's cold outside."

"Yes, Daddy." I could hear the teasing in her voice.

"Call me that later tonight and see if you don't get your fine ass spanked real good."

She moaned. "Please?"

"Fuck. Stop that, wicked thing." I sat back up and sucked in a breath. "See you soon, baby."

She said her goodbye, and I dropped the call and took it all in.

Life was different, and I would love her differently than I loved Laila, but something told me over time it would be a bigger love, a greater one. I knew what I'd lost the first time, and if that type of love existed with Bailey, there was no way in hell I was losing it again.

"Okay. So let me get this straight," Bailey said from the backseat. "I'm making the list, and then we'll reorganize it into the order of which toy you want the most?"

I glanced up into the rearview mirror as she looked down at Austin, who was tucked against her and strapped down in the middle seat even though the other full-sized seat was available. My chest tightened, and I shoved back the need to tear up. He liked her. I loved her.

How fucking blessed we were.

"Hey," my sister whispered as she put her hand on my arm. "It's okay."

"I know." I smiled and turned back to the traffic ahead of us as Austin updated Bailey on just how detailed she needed to be as his personal elf for the trip. The kid was beyond excited.

We got to the first store and walked to the door as snow danced around us all. I reached out and took Bailey's hand, lifting it to my lips and kissed the back of it as she smiled up at me.

"Thank you."

"For?" She squeezed my hand and wrapped her other hand around my bicep as she pressed her cheek against me.

"For playing along with him."

"I'm not playing along. I'm excited. I love kids." She released my hand and moved up to Nina and Austin. "I need my notepad, Sir."

"Oh yeah!" Austin handed it to her and reached out to take her hand.

Nina moved back to walk beside me as Bailey and Austin skipped toward the store. "Well, damn. I think we've been replaced, Bubba."

"I think so." I wrapped an arm around her shoulders. "You think there's enough snow at the house to make a snowman this afternoon?"

"The weatherman this morning said that we should be about knee deep in snow by five tonight. I'm thinking you and Bailey should put up a Christmas tree with Aus."

"Oh, I don't know, Nina." I released her and held the door open. "You know that damn tree still gets me right in the middle of the chest."

My sister turned and placed her hand over my heart. "And it's been two years. Austin deserves to start getting pieces of his holidays back, Jer."

I nodded. "You're right. Yeah, okay. We can get a tree. We'll stop on the way home and cut one down. We can make a big deal out of it."

A big smile covered my sister's face. "I'll get a basket and pick out some decorations while he's looking at toys. We can surprise him."

"Alright. Let's do it." I left her to her giddiness over the damn tree and went in search of my family. I stopped beside the aisle to find Bailey on her knees as Austin rattled off different toys, taking the time to show her each one as if she needed a visual to get the list right.

I leaned against the end-cap and took the moment in deep.

"You know that we didn't used to do this." Austin smiled over at Bailey, who was about the same height as him on her knees. "My daddy started it two years ago."

"Oh yeah?" Bailey's sweet voice pulled at my heart. "I like it. I think everyone should do it."

"Me too." Austin nodded and stared at my girl. "He did it to help me not be sad at Christmas."

"I like that your daddy has a big heart." She reached out and touched the side of Austin's face. "You have the same heart as he does, right?"

"I think so." He glanced down at his shirt and back up. "Well, maybe not the exact same heart."

Bailey laughed, and I could hear the tears in the sweet sound. "I think it's okay to be sad when you want to be. Even at Christmas. You just be you, okay?"

He nodded and turned back to the toys. "I'm not as sad as I used to be, but sometimes my chest still hurts."

Tears filled my eyes and dripped over to my cheeks as my heart broke in my chest. I needed to have more open talks with the kiddo about Laila.

"Well, I think we should put up a Christmas tree soon, and at the top, we can put a beautiful angel for your mom. What do you think about that?"

He smiled and turned to Bailey. "I like it! She would love that. I want a tree! Can we really?"

She fell back on her butt as he plowed into her with a big hug.

I wiped my eyes and my nose and moved over to help pull them up as the three of us laughed.

"What are you two doing?" I gave them both a look as I put them back on their feet.

They laughed harder, and Austin wrapped his arms around Bailey's waist and pressed his cheek to her hip. "Bailey said I could get a tree, Daddy. Please?"

"That okay?" Concern moved across her beautiful face, and I wanted to reach out and pull her into a long kiss, but I needed to be careful around Austin.

"Oh yeah. Nina is already running around this place getting decorations for us."

"Yay!" Austin bounced on his feet. "I want to help."

Nina pulled up on the side of our aisle and wagged her eyebrows. "Let's go kiddo. Get into the buggy and hold on tight."

"Nina." I gave her a look as Austin ran to her and she put him in the front of the cart. "Be careful."

"He's five. Get over it." She took off, and the sound of Austin screaming his head off in joy filled the store.

I turned and reached for Bailey. "Get over here."

"Am I in trouble?" She pressed her hands to my chest, one still holding the notebook and pen.

"No. Not unless you want to be." I leaned down and brushed my lips by hers. "Where did you come from, Bailey? Right when I thought I'd spend the rest of my life on shitty blind dates, there you were."

"I come from here." She smiled and lifted to her toes.

I kissed her long and hard, putting every bit of my thanks, my desire, my hunger for the sweet woman into my attack.

"Wow," she whispered and gripped my shirt with her free hand as she wobbled on her feet. "More of that please?"

"Oh yeah. Tonight. After the tree and stuff. We'll put Austin to bed and then lots more of that." I kissed her again and wrapped my arm around her shoulders as we went to find Austin.

It wasn't hard. You could hear him yelling in delight from a mile away. The sound was music to my ears and a balm to my soul.

20

BAILEY

"How is that?" I moved back and glanced down at Austin, seeking his approval.

He put his hands on his little hips and tilted his head to the side as he studied the tree. "Oh yeah. I like that a lot. We need a few more candy canes, and it should be perfect."

We had stopped by the Christmas tree lot just outside of the city and cut down the perfect tree for Jeremy's living room. It almost touched the ceiling, but not quite.

It had been an emotionally stressful day seeing that the holidays had to be so damn hard on Austin and Jer. I had witnessed the heaviness coming off of both of them, and more than anything else, I wanted to solve it. I wanted to take it away, but to do so would be to ask them to forget their pain, to forget Laila existed.

It was unfair to them to even think about it.

"Daddy?" Austin glanced back.

I turned to find Jeremy sitting on the couch, watching us. His big, strong shoulders were rolled in a little, and his expression sad.

"I like it. It's beautiful." He straightened up once our attention was on him. "You need me to put the angel you guys got on the top?"

"Yeah. It's for Mommy." Austin knelt down to grab the angel. "You think she would like it?"

Jeremy stood and gave what looked like a forced smile. "Oh yeah. She would love it. Let me see, and I'll get it up there for us."

Austin handed it over and moved over to me.

I reached down and picked the little guy up without thinking much about it. He was probably bordering too big to be carried around, but I didn't care.

"Let me grab my ladder." Jeremy turned and walked toward the garage door on the side of the kitchen without looking at either one of us.

I moved over to the couch and sat down, pulling Austin fully into my lap. "We need to write your Santa letter. You know that, right?"

"We still have a week until Christmas." He glanced up at me as he pressed his little cheek to my shoulder.

"Yeah, but we gotta mail it to the North Pole. Come on, man. You don't know how this works?" I used a funny voice and crinkled my nose.

He laughed and wrapped his arms around me. "Can I tell you something?"

"Anything." I leaned down and kissed his forehead, feeling more comfortable with him than I did with Rhys or Jeremy.

"Do you think you and my daddy will get married? Like, maybe you could be my mom?" His voice diminished to nothing more than a soft whisper.

"I don't know, sweetheart. I love your daddy a lot, but sometimes dating is a messy thing."

"Like making pancakes?" He blinked a few times and squeezed me tighter.

Jeremy walked back in and put the ladder up. "What are you two turkey's whispering about?"

"Nun-ya," I responded and smiled down at Austin.

"What's Nun-ya?" he asked.

Jeremy laughed and glanced down at us from the top of the ladder.

"It means, 'Nun-ya' business. None of your business." He gave me a look. "Stop teaching him to be bad."

I laughed. "I'm not teaching him that. We were talking about pancakes."

"Yeah right." Jeremy turned and put the angel on the tree.

"We were, Daddy!" Austin sat up.

I rubbed his back as we watched Jeremy finish getting the tree topper on.

"You like it?" Jer turned and smiled down at us. "Is it straight?"

"It's perfect." Austin got up and walked toward the tree. "Mommy would love it."

"She sure would, Buddy." Jeremy climbed back down the ladder and knelt in front of Austin. "Okay, Mister. Bedtime. Go brush your teeth and holler when you're ready for me to tuck you in."

"Can Bailey tuck me in with you?" He glanced over his shoulder and lifted his thumb toward me.

I laughed as Jeremy assured him that I could come too. Austin bounded off, and I stood.

"I'm proud of you," I said as I walked toward him.

"That so?" He wrapped his strong arms around me and leaned down to kiss me softly several times.

"Yes. I know today was hard. I'd take every bit of it from you if I could." I leaned against him, enjoying his strength and the peace I found in his arms.

"I would never give that to you or anyone else." He cupped my face and studied me. "But it means the world to me that you'd take it. Let's get Aus in bed and take some time for each other."

"I'd like that." I pressed upward and kissed him in a way that I knew would let him know just how badly I wanted to take care of him.

"Hot," he whispered against my lips. "So naughty."

"And I need a spanking." I smiled, kissed him again and turned as Austin yelled that he was ready.

We tucked the little guy in and walked back to Jeremy's bedroom. I turned to face him and pulled my t-shirt off as I walked backwards down the long hall.

"More," he commanded.

I undid my bra and flung it into the spare bedroom.

"Your jeans. Face away from me." He walked into the bedroom behind me and closed the door.

After turning around, I undid my jeans and slid them and my panties down my legs as I bent over slowly.

A groan ripped from me as he knelt behind me and gripped my thighs. He wasted no time pressing his mouth to my pussy and using his strong hands to massage my ass.

"Jeremy," I whispered roughly as I glanced up and reached for the edge of the bed. I gripped it with both hands and closed my eyes as he rolled his tongue through my folds and sucked at my sensitive skin. My legs shook as he ran his thumbs over my asshole, pressing in a little, but nothing more than a good tease.

A full sized mirror was on the wall to my left as I glanced over there. Seeing him kneeling behind me, his huge body locked in place, muscles bunched and me naked, bent over, beckoning to whatever he wanted was enough to fling me off the edge of sanity.

I screamed and pressed back. He groaned and worked me with slow torturous licks.

"Please fuck me," I moaned and arched my back as he stood and ran his hands up my back, pressing in and gripping my sides greedily.

"All night, baby." He patted my ass and glanced over at the mirror with a naughty smile on his lips. "Like watching us?"

"It's such a turn on." I locked eyes with him in the mirror and watched as he pulled his shirt over his head and kicked off his jeans. He was going commando, so no need to strip off any underwear. His dick was thick and fully alert. My mouth watered to see it glistening at the tip.

"I'll get a condom in a minute." He gripped himself and stroked a few times before moving up behind me.

I shook with anticipation as I watched him bend his knees a little. His legs were beyond sexy. So strong and well developed.

126

A moan rolled through me as the thick tip of his cock pressed against my ass, pulling down as he moved down to my pussy in a slow movement.

"God, you're so fucking hot, Bailey." He ran his hand up my back and gripped the back of my neck as he rimmed my entrance, pushing in a little and pulling up on his cock to create pressure.

"Don't tease me tonight. I need to feel you inside of me." I gripped the sheets and turned back toward the bed to let my head drop.

"You're not in charge, Angel, so hush." He pulled his cock out and back up to my ass.

I pressed back, wanting to know how much of him I could fit inside of me. Pain raced through my back, and I moved forward and cried out.

He popped my ass and growled. A warning. "Stay still and let me explore you. Yes?"

"Yes," I mumbled and let out a long whimper as he rimmed my asshole again, pressing in a little and pulling down, stretching me.

"I love the way your body opens up for me, baby. You should see how wet you are."

"I can feel it," I murmured as he slid his cock back down to my pussy and played his game a few more times.

By the time he gave me a few inches, I was testy and shaking hard. A growl ripped from my lips as I jerked my head back. "Enough!"

He smiled and slapped my ass hard. "Get on that bed, and I'll fuck you the way you want to be fucked. After you come, I'm taking my goddamn time, though. Bossy bitch."

I smiled and got on the bed, my knees pressed to the edge, my shins hanging over. I pressed back until my stomach was against my thighs and my ass hung over the edge far. "Thank you."

"Don't thank me yet." He walked up as I turned my face to watch him in the mirror again.

He gripped the back of my neck hard and my right ass cheek with his free hand. "You want this dick? You get it."

"Please?" I lifted up a little as he pressed into me with one hard thrust. The moan that filled the air around me was slutty, need, relieved.

"No need to be nice now." He rocked against me, fucking me with deep, short thrusts. "Your ass is on the naughty list for sure."

I laughed and bounced back a little, fucking myself on his massive cock. Another orgasm swelled in my stomach but didn't hit until he pressed his thumb into my ass and gripped my cheek with the rest of his fingers.

"God," I mumbled and rolled my hips, enjoying the sensation of him tucked into both of my holes.

"Yeah, sweet girl. Fuck yourself on everything I'm offering you." He leaned over a little farther and wrapped his hand around the side of my head, his fingers pressing to my lips. "Suck on them like you would this big dick you like having in your mouth."

I moaned loudly and pulled his fingers into my mouth. The sound and scent of our fucking left me trembling with need. My orgasm hit full force a moment later, but Jeremy didn't let up. He pressed his dick deep into my sloppy wetness, his thick thumb faster in my ass, and his fingers fully into my mouth.

"I'm gonna come, Bailey. You're too much, baby. Let me get a cond-"

I bit his fingers as I rocked through my orgasm, my thoughts lost to pleasure.

"Ouch! Damn." He fucked me harder as if angry with me. "Fine. Don't say shit to me later when you're carrying my baby."

I moaned again and opened my mouth. He pulled his fingers out of my mouth and gripped my hair as he jack-hammered my pussy and worked my ass open.

"I got on the pill," I whispered through the lusty haze.

"Such a good girl." He pulled out and removed his hand from me. "Let's be safe just in case."

"How-" I cried out as he pressed the head of his cock to my ass. "Take what you can, but be careful."

I pressed back against him as my body lit on fire. Never in a million years had I experienced anything so good.

He reached around and gripped my breasts, pulling at my nipples as he bit along the top of my back. "I'm so close. Squeeze me real good with that tight ass, and I'm going to unload inside of you, Bailey."

I whimpered at the thought and pressed back before milking a few inches of his cock over and over.

"That's it," he moaned against the back of my neck as deliciously hot come filled my ass with each additional thrust.

"So good," I moaned and pulled at his dick with my body until he forced me to stop.

Jeremy moved back and held onto my ass cheek. "Fuck me. That was incredible."

"I'll grab a towel."

"No. Come get in the bath with me." He patted my ass and walked to the bathroom. "Let me hold you and then we'll get in bed together and do it all over again."

"Hell yes." I got up and walked to the bathroom, my body sore, but my appetite was high. I wanted more. I wanted everything he was willing to give me.

He turned on the bath water and reached for me, pulling me flush against him. The firm press of his strong chest against my breasts felt so fucking good, so right.

"You're drowning me in lust and love, B. Is that what you wanted to do?" He brushed my hair back and leaned down to kiss me a few times.

B. He hadn't called me B since we were kids. It was the nickname he gave me when he and Jeremy first became friends in Junior High.

I smiled up at him and wrapped my arms around him. "I just want you to love me."

"Too late, sweet girl. You're behind the curve by a few weeks." He kissed me until the bathtub was ready. We got in him in the back and me in front. I pressed my hand against his strong cheek and relaxed against him while he washed my chest and promised me the world.

I wanted to offer it back to him, but I had one hurdle to overcome, and it was a big one.

His mother.

21

JEREMY

ONE WEEK LATER

The week leading up to Christmas was a juggle and a half. With Austin out of school and everyone wanting to have a fucking holiday party, I was aching to spend time with Bailey. She seemed to be having the same craziness in her own world. I needed our lives blended sooner rather than later. I wanted her beside me.

"What's up, man? Merry Christmas Eve!" Rhys's voice filled up my ear as I pressed the phone to it and paced out in front of the fire station.

"Hey. Yeah, you too man. Everything going okay down there? I heard you guys were having some serious-ass weather." I glanced up toward the sky and took a deep breath in. The cold felt good against my face after a hot shower.

"Oh yeah. How's everything there? My sister doing okay? You're being good to her right, man? Hate to have to fuck you up. You're one of my *only* friends."

I chuckled and glanced down at the snow. "You *are* my only friend."

"I take that as a yes?"

"Yeah. She's doing so good." I turned toward the firehouse and ran my hand down my face.

"What's wrong?"

"I'm in love with her, Rhys. Like, I got that shit bad."

"And you're sure It's not a rebound, cause maybe with you not letting anyone in over the last two years, your emotions are just high strung from *not* being used. You know what I'm saying?"

I nodded as if the fucker could see me. "Yes. I understand, and I've been trying to figure that out. I want her with me all the time. I'm so smitten with her it's a little sickening."

He laughed. "She's a really good woman, Jer. Just like Laila was."

Laila. The sound of her name on Rhys's lips would have caused me to almost double over in pain a few months back, but now it was a dull ache.

"Do you think," I paused and turned back to the street as my heart hammered in my chest, "Do you think that it would be okay to move past mourning? It's been two years."

"It's been two fucking years. Do you hear yourself?"

I took a deep breath. "Dude. You know what she meant to me. I built my world around her. She was the air I breathed, my life, my joy, my everything."

"And she's gone, man. And you're still here. And you're so fucking strong." I could hear him choking up. My eyes filled with tears. "You can do this, Jeremy. Move on. Say goodbye and move on. You ain't ever gotta forget. You hear me."

I nodded again as I pressed my fingers to my eyes. "But it's time."

He sniffled. "Yeah, man. It's time. Go say goodbye. You want me to fly my fat ass down there, and we'll do it together?"

I laughed as a sob crept up my chest. "No. I'm ready. I just needed someone to tell me it was alright to do it."

"Well, you non-leader mother fucker... it's time to do it."

"I follow Jesus and Tony Robbins, man. That's about all I got in the follower category."

He laughed. "I know that. I'm just picking on you. Take care of it and then wrap your life around my sister's. She's gonna love you more than any other woman ever would. You've been her *Laila* for a long time, Jer."

He was right. I wasn't telling him that he was right, but he was.

"Merry Christmas, brother." I listened to him repeat it and dropped the call. A quick text to Bailey to make sure I was going home to her later that night and I was on my bike, headed toward the cemetery.

I took the long way, going fast on the straight-away and slowing down on the curves. I had so much to live for again. My sweet little guy who would grow up into a strong man that loved as deeply as I did, and my girl. My woman. My soon to be everything.

Marry me.

It wouldn't be long until I asked her. I couldn't hold back now that I knew. I wasn't interested in a long, pseudo courtship. I wanted her coffee mug next to mine by the sink and her toothbrush in the holder beside mine. I wanted her shit all over the house, her panties on my floor and her warm, soft body to wake up next to each morning.

I needed to hear her whisper my name in the dead of night when she had a nightmare and to feel her hips thrust forward as I pressed my erection against her perfect ass before the sun came up.

No fucking way I was waiting and biding my time for those things. She loved me already, and I was completely lost to her. There were only a few things left to do before I bought a ring.

Talk to her dad.

Talk to my mom.

Say goodbye to my Laila.

I turned into the cemetery and parked by the church seeing that there were no direct paths to the gravestones. The snow was thick and a little higher than ankle deep, but I had on big shit-kicker boots. There was nothing to worry about.

My phone buzzed, and I pulled it out to see Nina had texted me. But it wasn't Nina.

Nina: Daddy. It's Austin.

I laughed. Who else would call me daddy from Nina's phone?

Me: Hey buddy. I'm heading home soon. Bailey is coming over, and then we'll probably go see Granny for a little while tonight.

Nina/Austin: Ok, but it's Christmas Eve. We gotta get milk out and cookies made. Is there time, or should you stop and get cookies? I'm not sure if Santa likes the stuff from the store. Does he?

Me: He's Santa. He eats all cookies and drinks all milk, but I should be home in time to make cookies.

Nina/Austin: Good. Sugar cookies are his favorite. With white icing and red hots. Get the stuff before you get home, and we'll make them together.

Me: How do you know that's his favorite?

I held my breath as I walked to Laila's grave. Had Austin figured out that I was Santa? Fuck. I hoped not. He was growing up too fast as it were.

Nina/Austin: Duh. He eats every bit of them and licks up the crumbs.

I laughed hard and responded that I'd get the stuff. After tucking my phone back into my pocket, I knelt in front of the tombstone that I'd shed so many tears over. Running my hand over the top, I sucked in the icy air around me.

"Laila. It's me." I smiled and glanced up toward the heavens. "I wish you were here, baby. You'd love how sassy Austin is. He reminds me more and more of you each day."

I waited for the tears, but they didn't come. I was forever grateful for the sense of peace and rightness over the moment.

"We got him a tree this year. It was my girlfriend's idea." I took a shaky breath and gripped the tombstone. "I gotta let you go now, baby. It's been a long two years of looking everywhere for you, but

Rhys is right. You're not coming back. Austin and I will see you again one day. I know we will, baby. But until then, I have to move on, and I found someone that Austin likes, and I love. I think you'd love her too. It's Rhys's little sister, Bailey. She's got a good heart. She's going to take care of us both, me and Austin."

Tears pooled in my eyes as I stood up.

"I love you. I'll always love you. I just have to learn how to love me again too." I stood there for a long time letting the icy wind of winter slam against me. I expected a breakdown or something more than the few tears that dripped down my cheeks. My life would never be the same again without her in it, but I was starting to see that maybe it didn't have to be the same. Maybe it could be just as good, but different.

I turned and walked back toward my bike as an older gentleman walked past me with a handful of red roses in his hands. He glanced up and smiled.

"Mighty cold out here, hm son?"

"Sure is, Sir." I stopped and smiled at him. "Those are going to be beautiful against the snow."

"Yeah. Sarah loved red roses." He pulled them up to his face and breathed in deeply. "Forty years of marriage and I lost her last year."

"I'm so sorry." I crossed my arms over my chest. "I lost my wife two years ago to a car accident."

"I'm sorry too then." He gave me a warm smile. "Two years is a long time to grieve for most, but you take the time you need. When you come out of it, you'll be thankful you did."

"Thanks. Merry Christmas to you." I extended my hand and shook his as he winked.

"You too. Take care."

I turned and walked back to my bike. Forty years of marriage. I wanted that with Bailey. I was thirty-two then and would be seventy-two when we celebrated such a big number. It was possible, and some part of me had already started planning it all out. I got on the bike and breathed in deeply. Letting go of the past was damn near impossible, but sometimes the future compelled you to do just that.

Marry me.

I started the bike and pulled my phone from my pocket as it buzzed with a special vibration I had for the fire station. They were gearing up for a fire and were a man short. I texted back to grab my shit and give me the address. I would meet them there.

After getting over to the side of town where the flames were licking up toward the sky, I called Bailey. She answered on the first ring.

"Hi, baby."

"Hey." I repositioned the phone as I got off my bike. "Hey look, I had to come help with a fire. The guys are running a man short."

"Oh no."

"Yeah, and it's Christmas Eve. Can you please go over to my place and make cookies with Austin? I'd ask Nina, but I think she has some big fancy party that her and Mom are going to tonight. They always try to get me to go too, but it's just not my thing."

"Of course. What kind of cookies does Santa like?" I could hear the teasing in her voice. God, I loved this woman.

I wanted to fling a million flirty, naughty things at her, but the situation in front of me was screaming for my attention. "Sugar cookies. White icing. Sprinkles and red hots. Austin loves to cut them out and decorate them. I'll be home as soon as I can. Tell him what happened?"

"I'm getting dressed and heading over there now. I have a stocking for him to decorate and I bought a Christmas movie too. We'll have a great time together. Just be safe, Jeremy."

"I will." I dropped the call though I wanted to tell her that I loved her. I'd already hinted at it or basically said something close to it several times, but she needed to know the truth. Some part of me loved her because she was Rhys's little sister, a sweet tomboy from my past that I knew in the depths of my soul was my second chance. Another part wanted to love her because she reminded me of high school, my hometown, of Laila and every warm memory that I had.

But even more than all of that. I loved her because she was her, and it stunned me how much she loved me.

BAILEY

CHRISTMAS EVE

I got off the phone with Jeremy and gathered up everything for Christmas Eve over at his place. I'd bought him and Austin several things that I had originally planned to take over the next morning.

A knock at my door had me cursing. I'd forgotten that I'd invited Ellen over for a Christmas Eve night of fun.

She smiled as I opened the door and held up a bottle of wine. "Merry Christmas to you!"

I laughed and pulled her into a hug. "I gotta go over to Jeremy's. He's at a fire right now, and his little guy doesn't have anyone to spend Christmas Eve with."

"Awesome." She put the wine down and held up candy canes. "Can I come?"

"Oh yeah. Of course." I moved back and walked to the kitchen. "Let's get everything packed up and then we'll go by the grocery store and get stuff for sugar cookies."

"Oh! I love sugar cookies. The ones you cut out and decorate?" Her eyes grew wide as I shoved all the presents for the boys into a laundry basket.

"Yep. We're going to make a dozen or so tonight." I stood.

"What can I get?" She walked to the kitchen and picked up the bag I had puzzles and stocking making stuff in. "This?"

"Yes. Let's go." I grabbed my coat, the presents, and my purse. "Hopefully the fire isn't too bad. It always throws me for a loop that anything would be *able* to burn in this weather. It's freezing outside."

"Stranger things have happened." She closed the door behind us and reached for the keys to lock it as I handed them off to her. "So, how's your brother?"

I smiled. "He's doing good. He asked about you today too."

"He did?" She bounced on her toes and then tried to play it cool. "I mean," she lowered her voice and shrugged, "he did?"

I laughed loudly. "You're so stupid. It's one of the reasons I love you."

She moved up beside me as we took the stairs down to the parking lot. "What did he say."

I cleared my throat in a very dramatic manner and glanced at her with my eyebrows lifted. "How. Is. Ellen?"

"Ugh." She popped me with her free hand and rolled her eyes. "You are *no* fun at all."

"That's not what Jeremy says." I chuckled and walked to the car. The snow was hellacious, which was no fun at all to drive in.

"TMI." She got into the car and buckled up.

I got in and glanced over at her. "So, have you not seen anyone since Rhys left?"

"Sort of." She leaned back and let out a sigh. "Your brother is just so big and manly. Now, everyone I go out with feels like Pee-Wee Herman compared to Rhys. It's disturbing."

"He is huge." I pulled out of the parking lot and drove to the store as she jabbered on about guys in general. I had to stop her when she tried to talk about cock sizes and how my brother compared. That was where I drew the line, and drew it deep in the sand.

"Alright." She lifted her hands as we pulled up to Jeremy's place.

"Weird. Where is Nina?" I got out of the car and jogged up the stairs to knock on the door. After standing there for a minute, freezing my ass off, I texted Nina.

"Where are they?" Ellen got out of the car and hollered up at me.

"They're at Jeremy's mom's house. Nina didn't know I was coming, so she took Austin over there. No biggie. We'll just go over there." I turned and bounded down the stairs, almost busting my ass as I did.

"Be careful!" Ellen yelled and covered her face.

I laughed. "Wow. Thanks a lot."

"What? I hate seeing people get hurt." She got back into the car and huffed. "Why didn't someone tell you that they were at Jeremy's mom's house?"

"Because Nina didn't know, and Jeremy is fighting a fire. Let's go get the kiddo and come back over here. I don't really like Jeremy's mom much. She looks at me like I'm a floozy from the titty bar."

Ellen laughed. "She doesn't know you at all then."

"Nor does she care to."

"Shame." She turned and looked out the window.

I enjoyed the silence on the way over to Jeremy's mother's big ass house. It was beautiful but so odd for the northeast. I wanted to ask Jeremy about it. Maybe his mom was from Louisiana or something. The house was perfect for the outskirts of New Orleans, but up in New Hampshire, it just seemed off.

"You want me to wait here?" Ellen glanced up from her phone as I parked in front of the giant house.

"Sure. Yeah." I unbuckled and got out. After pulling my coat tighter and zipping it up, I walked up the long flight of stairs to the front door, took a deep breath and rang the doorbell.

I had no doubt that Ms. Bennett wasn't going to be thrilled to see me on her porch. Not that I'd ever done shit to her, but she was upper class and didn't think I was right for Jeremy. Maybe I'd get lucky, and Nina would answer the door.

"Jeremy isn't here." She opened the door, gave me a blank expression and started to close the door.

I reached out and put my hand against it. "I'm here to pick up Austin. Jeremy had to run out to a fire and asked me to get Austin and take him back to the house."

"He didn't text me." She opened the door a little and narrowed her eyes. "I'll text Nina and see what she says. She took him down the street to Katie's house to exchange gifts."

"Okay. Sure." I reached up to keep her from shutting the door, again. "Can I come in and wait or do you want me to wait in my car? It's too cold to wait out here."

The woman had a way of making me feel completely worthless. She turned and left the door open as she pulled her phone toward her face. Why did she hate me so much? Was she like this to everyone Jeremy dated or wanted to date? Was she like this to Laila?

"Well. It seems you're right." His mother turned and pressed her hip against the counter in the kitchen. "Nina confirmed your claims."

I nodded and turned away from her. "The house looks beautiful. You did a great job decorating."

"Don't be silly, child. I didn't decorate this place. Could you see a sixty-year-old woman in heels getting up on a ladder?"

I turned and smiled, thinking that maybe she was being funny, but she wasn't. She was chastising me.

"Um, no. No. I just-"

"Don't stutter. It shows your ignorance." She walked past me and brushed her shoulder against mine.

Anger and sadness swirled in the pit of my stomach. How much of a chance did I really have with Jer if his mom thought I was a piece of shit? None. He loved her and cared about her and Nina. What did Nina think about me?

"Mrs. Bennett." I turned and called to her before I realized what I was doing.

"What?" Her tone was clipped and filled with agitation.

"Have I done something to offend you?"

"You being here offends me." She crossed her narrow arms over her chest and lifted her eyebrow. "Jeremy is the only male child I have and is heir to a lot of money. As his mother, it's my responsibility to make sure that whoever he marries next is worthy of that treasure."

"And you approved of Laila?" I crossed my arms over my chest and forced myself to stand my ground. There was no way I was going to break down and cry in front of the old witch. At least, I hoped I didn't.

She snorted in disgust. "Not even close. She was riff-raff too. All of you were and are. Rhys included. You come from poor families with pitiful tastes, childish traditions, and pathetic backings. It's honestly infantile for you to think for a second that Jeremy could truly be interested in a plain-Jane girl like you." She took a few steps toward me, and fuck if I didn't want to back up.

Never enough.

"You don't even know my family." I stood my ground. "Or how long I've had feelings for Jeremy."

"Nor do I care." She stopped right in front of me and leaned down. "You, my dear, are a rebound. He's going to love you until he doesn't. The poor boy is still lost in grief over his pitiful choice of a wife from the first go-around. He's nothing like me, but a bit like his father. He loves a good piece of ass, and often confuses that lust for sex for love."

"What?" I stepped back like I'd been slapped. Tears filled my eyes. "I'm a good person."

"Says who? You?" She laughed and pointed to the door. "Get out. Don't come back. Wait on the porch for Austin, and if you let anything happen to him, you will regret it."

She turned and walked toward the living room, leaving me there with tears dripping down my face. Never in a million years had I been treated so badly. Never. Not ever.

I half ran to the door and out onto the porch. I turned to it with it still cracked as if I were saying goodbye and wiped up my tears. No fucking way I was letting anyone see me cry over being cut down by Jeremy's mother, though I was mortified by it.

"Bailey!" Austin's voice caused me to suck it up and turn.

I knelt and swooped him up in my arms as he laughed. "Hi, Buddy. I hear you need a cookie-baking elf to help you tonight."

"I do!" He laughed and clung to me.

"Hey. You okay?" Nina stopped in front of me, her face filled with worry.

I put Austin down and patted his back. "Go get in the backseat, little man. Ellen is in there and we have candy canes and Christmas music already on for you."

"Yes!" He hugged Nina tightly and turned, jogging down the stairs as best he could all wrapped up in his winter coat and boots.

"I'm okay. Just some stuff I'm dealing with from home." I reached up and wiped at my eyes. "It's all good."

"You sure?" She pulled me into a tight hug. "I don't like to see you crying."

"Yeah, well, I'm a girl. It happens from time to time." I moved back and forced a smile. "I'll see you tomorrow maybe?"

"Yep. We're all supposed to be over at Jer's around ten for breakfast and presents. I'll bring mom and the gifts then."

I nodded before turning to go. "Sounds great. Merry Christmas, Nina."

"You too!" She walked into the house as I made my way back to the car.

There was no way I was going to move things forward with Jeremy without first talking to him about the situation with his mother. I couldn't stand the thought of falling even more deeply in love with him only to have him shut me down because of her. He might say that wasn't a possibility, but I knew their relationship... he listened to her just like I listened to my folks, only my parents weren't evil dark bitches.

At least not most of the time.

23

JEREMY

CHRISTMAS DAY

I let out a long sigh of relief as I pulled up to the house early on Christmas morning. Bailey's car was parked in the snow, and the idea of her being in the house asleep in my bed had my pulse spiking.

There was nothing I wanted more than to fall into the bed face-first and pass out, but knowing she was there, that wasn't going to happen. Making love to her for a little while was first on my list of priorities.

I got out of the car and walked up to the house as the sun started to rise behind me. There was a slim chance Austin wasn't going to be up and hopping around the tree in the next hour, but I was praying for a quick fuck and a quicker nap if at all possible.

The house was completely silent when I walked in, and the scent of sugar cookies filled my senses. I walked to the kitchen to find a note scribbled in Austin's handwriting and another one beside it from Santa. I picked it up and smiled, realizing that Bailey must have written it for my son.

The cookies were half eaten, and the milk was all gone.

I stopped by the living room as my heart overflowed with love and adoration for the beautiful woman I was soon to ask to be my wife. She hadn't left anything undone. A huge fire truck sat in front of the tree with a teddy bear laying across it as if the little bastard was sound asleep.

I laughed as tears filled my eyes. How in the world could a cold-hearted asshole like me find another woman like her? She was everything I dreamed I would find in my first chance love, but so much more than I hoped for in my second.

My phone buzzed, and I pulled it out to see Nina calling.

"Merry Christmas," I half-whispered into the phone.

"You didn't text me at midnight like you usually do." She sounded a little let down about it.

"Yeah, I'm sorry, Sis. I am honestly just walking into the house right now." I sat down on the couch and smiled as I realized Bailey finished wrapping all my presents and got them under the tree. There was no way she found the necklace I'd bought for her. It was high in my closet, just in case.

"Oh. Jeez. I'm so sorry, Jer."

"It's all good. We got the fire out about four this morning, and there was no loss of life. We're all good." I leaned back and ran my fingers through my wet hair. I was cold and tired. The only thing I wanted for Christmas was about an hour wrapped around my woman in the warmth of my covers.

"That's great news." Nina stopped talking, and the pregnant pause between us left me a little worried.

"What's up? You have something you want to say. Say it." I got back up and walked down the hallway toward Austin's room. I pushed the door open to find Bailey wrapped around him, both of them breathing deeply.

My heart felt like it might flood with love for them both.

"Something happened last night, but I'm not sure what."

I turned away from the bedroom and closed the door. "I'm lost."

"I took Austin down to Katie's place and, I don't know, when I got back with him, Bailey was on the front porch in tears." She took a deep breath. "Something happened with her and Mom."

"What?" I walked into my bedroom and closed the door before pulling off my t-shirt and crawling into my bed. I planned on talking to my sister and then going back to Austin's room to carry B back to my bed. "What happened? Did you ask Momma?"

"No. She was upset about it being the holidays and not having Dad." She let out a sigh. "Have you talked to Bailey?"

"She's still asleep. I'll go wake her up here shortly. She did cookies with Aus, cleaned the damn house, wrapped everything, wrote him a Santa letter. The fucking list goes on and on, Sis." I laid back and pinched the bridge of my nose as exhaustion rolled over me.

"She's a good woman, Jer. One you need to keep."

"I plan to." I yawned loudly. "I went to Laila's grave yesterday before the fire and said goodbye."

"Oh, Bubba. Why didn't you tell me? I could have gone with you."

"I appreciate that, but I needed to do it on my own." I turned on my side and pulled the covers from the other side of the bed over me. "It was time, you know?"

"You gotta make some room in your heart for new things."

"And not be the damaged one anymore?" I smiled and pulled my pillow down farther.

"You never were damaged, Jeremy. Just dented a little, but something tells me that Rhys's little sister is going to help heal all of those dents. Her, Austin and some time." My sister made more sense than anyone else in my life did. She loved me with a patient love. It was something I cherished deep in my soul.

"I love you, Sis. I'm going to rest my eyes and then go talk to Bailey. I think I'll propose in the late spring after we've had the time to date a little longer and get to know each other a little better."

"That's a great idea. Mom and I will be over in a little while unless you don't want me to bring her. We don't *have* to be there today."

"Sure you do. It's Christmas. I'm sure whatever is going on, we can solve it. Mom loves me. If she's being a bitch, she's doing it out of some sense of needing to protect me. We'll figure it out. Merry Christmas."

"You too, Bubba. See you in a little while. Sleep well."

"Yeah." I dropped the call and closed my eyes as darkness rushed in to take me under.

Sleep. I just needed a little bit of sleep.

———————

"Daddy! Merry Christmas!" Austin jumped on the bed beside me, yelling at the top of his lungs.

"Hey man." I grabbed him and pulled him down to tickle him. "Why you gotta wake me up like that? Scared the hell out of me."

"No, it didn't." He wrestled me with all his might. He was full of energy. "Did you know that Santa came and ate all the cookies me and Bailey made last night?"

"I saw that when I came in this morning. Looked like he put your presents under the tree too." I lifted an eyebrow as he shrugged. "You totally saw it already, didn't you?"

"Yes! And guess what?"

"What's that?" I glanced toward the door, half-expecting Bailey to walk in any minute.

"This means that I'm not on the naughty list." He poked me in the chest over and over with his forefingers on each hand. "You were wrong! You were wrong-o!"

I laughed and pushed him off of me before rolling over and getting up. "Where is Bailey?"

"Um, I don't know." He got off the bed and shrugged his shoulders. "She laid down with me last night, but she wasn't in my bed when I got up."

"Hm. Well, you go check out your presents, and I'm going to solve the case of the missing girlfriend."

"Oh wow. She's your girlfriend now?" His eyes widened. "Dad. You know that girls have cooties."

"No, not when they get older. They slough those off like a snake does his skin." I gave him a knowing look and shook my head 'yes' at him.

"Really?" His eyes got wider. "Can you actually see it? The cootie skin?"

"Yep." I turned him around and sent him down the hallway with a head full of lies. "Bailey? Where you at, baby?"

Nothing. After checking every room in the house, I stopped in the kitchen and found a note by the coffee pot with my name on it. My stomach sank. Why would she leave a note and not stay to celebrate Christmas with us? We'd made plans to spend the whole damn day together.

I opened it and held my breath.

Merry Christmas Jer,

Just wanted to leave you a note to thank you for letting me spend the evening with Austin. We had a great time. I'm going to spend Christmas with Ellen and her folks. I know we made plans, but you enjoy your holiday with your sister and your mom. I have some thinking to do. I've been trying to talk to you about it for a little while now, but I never can figure out how to start the conversation.

It's just that you have a really bright future. You have a great family and an incredible career. You're older and just really well put together. You are set up to do some crazy awesome things. I think you should stop pushing against the grain and just accept the money that your father left for you, though it's none of my business. It would help you not to have to work so hard, and maybe you and Austin could take some trips together. He would love that!

Anyway. I'll catch up with you soon, and we can talk. I just think that maybe instead of settling for a plain girl like me who doesn't have her shit together and comes from nowhere that you should aim higher.

So, enjoy your Christmas, and I'll see you around.

146

Bailey

"No. No, no, no, no." The tear stains on the paper were still fresh. "Goddamnit no."

"Dad?" Austin came around the corner and skidded into the kitchen. "What's wrong?"

"Nothing." Horror raced through me. My stomach soured immediately, and with the lack of sleep I was running on, I wasn't going to be able to hold down my dinner.

"You sure?" He called after me as I jogged down the hallway and slammed the door to the bathroom. I barely made it to the toilet before I knelt and threw up everything inside of me.

No. No fucking way I was losing again. It wasn't happening. I didn't give a fuck what I had to do. There was no way Bailey was walking away from me. Not for the reasons she said on that piece of paper.

"Jeremy?" My sister's voice filled up the room as she knocked loudly on the door. "You okay? What's going on? We just got here, and Austin said you were sick."

I wiped my mouth and jerked the door open. Anger burned through me like never before. "What happened last night?"

My sister lifted her hands and took a step back. "I have no clue."

"What's going on?" My mother walked down the hallway.

"Bedroom. Now!" I yelled in a deep voice and walked to my room.

"Who?" Nina called after me.

"My. Mother." I walked into my room and pressed my hands to my stomach. A mixture of fury and disgust had me wanting to bend over again.

"What is the meaning of this?" She walked in and closed the door behind her.

I whirled around and lifted my fingers at her. "How dare you. You did this, didn't you? You did something to Bailey that has her running away from my goddamn life as fast as she can."

Mom lifted her hands and gave me a chastising look. "Now, Jeremy. You know as well as I do that she's just a rebound."

"No, the fuck she isn't," I barked and stood my ground. I wanted to cross the room and get in her face, but there was no way I was going to offend or hurt my own mother. I wasn't that kind of man. She'd pulled this same shit with Laila.

"Watch your language."

"You're going to find her, and you're going to apologize for being the meanest, black-hearted woman in the whole goddamn city. And you're going to do it right now, or catch this... you're going to leave this house, and me and Austin won't be a part of your life again. I've followed your silly rules and dating the series of sluts you sent me on dates with to make you happy." I locked my jaw as I shook in anger. "How dare you take away the only woman I can see me and Austin healing with. Do you hate me?"

"What? Of course not." She pressed her hands to her lips and let out a sob. "Why are you yelling at me?"

"What did you say to Bailey?" I forced myself to calm down just a little.

"I just told her the truth, son."

I pulled at my hair and let out a feral growl. "And what truth would that be?"

"That you're on the rebound." She lifted her hands toward me as I let out another deep, dark sound. "Jeremy. Stop that."

"You have two choices." I let out a long sigh and let my shoulders roll in. "My heart is breaking inside my chest like the day I stood at Laila's grave, and you've caused this. You can go fix it, or get out of my life. Forever."

"You're being-"

"Forever!" I screamed so loud the walls shook around me.

She took a step back and nodded. "I'll fix it. I'm sorry. I was only trying to do what was best for you."

"I'm thirty-two years old. You have no clue what's best for me." I ran my hands down my face. "You have until lunchtime today. I'm going to spend the morning with my son and my sister. Until this is righted, you're not welcomed in my house.

"Fine." She turned, flung my door open and marched back down the hallway. I had expected to hear her cry, but it wasn't her style. She barked something at Nina, spoke sweetly to Austin and I heard another door slam.

I sat down on the edge of my bed and pressed my face into my hands. I had to pull myself together. It was Christmas, and whether or not my mom did her part of setting things right - I would later that day.

I was in love with my best friend's baby sister, and she wasn't getting away from me that easily.

Not if I had something to say about it.

24

BAILEY

"What are you doing here on Christmas Day?" Tanner glanced up from the bar and smiled at me. "You had off, remember?"

"Yeah, but I had off at Thanksgiving too. I'm good. Seriously. My whole family is back in Illinois, and my mom and dad actually went to Hawaii to get out of the snow this year." I lifted my hands to the side and looked around. "This place is much better than moping around my empty apartment."

"Alright. Well, if you're going to be here," he smiled, "get your ass in gear."

I nodded, forced a smile and walked to the back. With one manager on duty, I would be playing bartender or waitress, one or the other. The events from the night before washed over me and crippled my resolve to keep my chin up.

Ducking into the employees' bathroom, I locked the door behind me and dropped down on the toilet. Why did what Jeremy's mother think matter so much to me? She wasn't the one I planned on marrying or having kids with.

A groan left me as I pressed my head into my hands. My heart hurt so bad I thought I might be sick.

I'd left him a fucking note instead of talking to him. What choice did I have?

My phone buzzed in my pocket, and I ignored it for a little while, but it finally got on my damn nerves. I assumed it might be Jeremy, but it was Rhys.

"Hey. Where you at? You trying to avoid your *only* sibling on Christmas? What the hell?" He sounded as full of life as he always did.

"No. I just-" I pursed my lips.

"Bailey? Are you crying?" His voice darkened.

"No. Yes. I don't know." I let out a sob and covered my eyes with my free hand. "Jeremy's mother hates me, and she made sure to let me know last night. I'm just a rebound, Rhys."

"Sis. Listen to me, that woman is evil. She tried to get rid of me and Laila. I promise you that her words are *not* Jeremy's. He just told me yesterday that he was falling in love with you. Please don't let her tear you guys apart." He let out a long sigh. "You just have to talk to Jeremy and stand up to her. She backs off when she realizes that you're not going anywhere."

"What if I am a rebound though? What if Jer thinks he's in love, but really it's just that he needs to start moving on, and I'm the first woman in sight when he takes that first step?"

"Not the case. I've already walked through all of this with him. He's my best friend. There's no way he would do anything like that to you. You know?"

"No." I sniffled loudly. "I don't know, and you know why?"

"Tell me why, boo."

"Because you don't know that you're dating a rebound until you find someone else more compatible or hot or wealthier that pulls you in an attraction toward them. Maybe he thinks he's falling in love, but when he finds someone better or more like Laila, he's going to walk. I can't do this, Rhys. Not with him. He's the man I've wanted all my life." I sniffled again. "Not a man like him, actually him. I've loved him since I was a little girl. I can't do this."

"Hey! Calm down, or I'm going to get my happy ass on a plane and bust his mouth open for upsetting you on Christmas. Now, take a deep breath."

I breathed in deeply and let out another sob as a fresh wave of tears came. I gave him my virginity, my gift. I handed it over without too much thought because it was him for shit's sake. Jeremy. My Jer. Rhys's Jer.

"Bailey." Rhys paused. "Where are you?"

"In the bathroom at work. I came in because I don't want to sit around my apartment and cry all fucking day. I can't do it." I reached up and wiped my eyes.

Someone knocked at the door, scaring me. "Bailey?"

"I gotta go," I mumbled into the phone. "Tanner, one of the managers, is at the door."

"Get yourself together and call me later. Promise?"

"Yes."

"Okay. I love you, Sis. Merry Christmas."

"You too." I dropped the call, splashed water on my face and opened the door.

Tanner was wide-eyed. "Hey, so there's an older lady in our office waiting for you." He reached out and gripped my shoulder. "You okay?"

"I don't know." I crossed my arms over my chest and walked toward the office. With my luck, Edward's true wife was there to scold me for going to an art even with her pervert of a husband. I could hear her calling me a hussy with each step I took.

Much to my surprise, it wasn't Edward's wife. It was Jeremy's mother.

"Bailey." She glanced up and smiled around me. "Thank you, Tanner. Can you close the door, please?"

"Yes, Ma'am." He closed the door, and I took a few steps back and pressed my back to it.

"It's Christmas," I said with an expressionless face. "Shouldn't you be with your family?"

"I need to apologize."

"I'm not interested. You're wasting your time. The damage is done.

I can't unhear or unfeel what you said to me. It's impossible." I shrugged and slipped my hand down into my apron pockets. "Jeremy does deserve better. You were right."

She nodded in a knowing way. "Yes. He deserves a better mother."

Her words surprised me a little. "What?" I asked.

"He deserves a better mother." She sat down on the chair closest to her and looked up at me. "When his father and I were dating, my mother was right in the middle of our relationship, constantly bothering both of us." She snorted and glanced down at her hands. "Henry was never good enough for my family." She looked back up. "We were rich, and he was poor, but they had no idea what a business mogul the man was going to grow to be, but I did."

"Henry was Jeremy's father?" I sat down and pushed my chair back, still wanting as much space as I could get between us.

"Yeah. He was everything to me." She laughed sadly. "I didn't marry him because of money or what I knew he would become." Her eyes filled with tears. "I married him because I fell so deeply in love with him, and to be somewhere without him felt like a funeral of sorts."

I nodded, encouraging her to go on.

"We grew into that love for our entire marriage, and I knew that he was my soul mate." She glanced back down at her hands as her voice broke a little. I'd never seen such a strong woman struggle with her words as I sat there and watched her. "His death was too much to bare." She glanced up as tears streaked down her cheeks.

I couldn't help but cry with her.

"He left us all the money in the world, but he took my heart with him when he went into the ground. There isn't another event in my lifetime that could tear my soul in half the way that day did. Standing at the head of his coffin as people apologized and went back to their lives was the worst day of my entire life."

She wiped her eyes and sniffled. I handed her a tissue.

"I'm so sorry, Ms. Bennett." I took a tissue and wiped at my eyes.

"No, child. I am. I didn't like Laila because she was a wild-ass who was in love with Jeremy and threatened to take him away from me, and in some ways, she did." She cleaned up her face before continuing.

"But the day she died, I watched my baby lose his soul too." She sniffled again as a fresh wave of tears slammed into both of us. "He stood at the front of her coffin as people said their 'I'm sorries', and his face aged, his skin paled, his chest deflated, and I knew-"

She was crying so hard that I was compelled to get up and move over to her. I knelt in front of her and wrapped my arms around her as she shook.

"I know Bailey that he too had died along with Laila. That he too would never fully breath again, just like I haven't since losing my Henry."

I brushed my hand over the back of her head and rubbed her back.

She reached up and wrapped me in a hug, standing and moving into my arms as she cried for a few more minutes.

"I'm so sorry," I whispered against her hair. I had no clue what else to say to her, but watching her hurt, hurt me so badly. I couldn't fathom losing Jeremy, and we were just starting our lives together. To have fostered and built that kind of love into an empire only to lose it was more than I could stand to even think about.

It was life-shattering.

"No. Honestly, Bailey." She moved back and reached for another tissue. "I'm sorry. I just wanted to push you as far away as I could, but it had nothing to do with you, dear. It was because I was scared that Jeremy would fall in love again only to have it ripped out of his fingers once more." She reached up and touched my cheek. "He wouldn't survive that. It's the reason I've never taken another husband. I can't do this again. I won't."

I understood completely, and with that knowledge, my chest relaxed, and my hurt dissipated.

"It's okay. Let's move past it because I can't imagine my life without Jeremy in it. I've loved him since I was a little girl, Ms. Bennett. He's been in my life because of Rhys since I was a kid." I moved back and wiped at my eyes. "I'll never stop loving him, and to have to do so from a distance-"

"Is a death of sorts too." She dropped her hands to the side, closed her eyes and let out a long sigh. "Forgive me for putting that on you. I only meant to protect him."

"Then why all the dates and pushing him to find a mother for Austin?" I blew my nose about the same time as she did. We smiled at each other and chuckled.

"Those women were absolutely whores. The worst girls I could find." She blotted her face with her fingers. "They were no threat at all, and my hope was that they would scare him off from women altogether, which worked just fine until fate put you right back in his life."

I smiled. "I love him so much. Leaving him a note this morning and walking away was the most difficult thing I've ever done."

"And you did it because I convinced you that *you* were not the best thing for him?"

"Yes." I nodded and let out a long sigh.

"Then I welcome you into my family, and will love you like I love my own children, but only if you can forgive me, Bailey. I was trying to protect my son, and I went about it in the most ignorant manner possible. By meddling in his damn love life."

"I forgive you." I nodded and forced a smile.

"Good. Come to my house with me then. We'll fix a big Christmas dinner and invite Nina, Austin, and Jeremy over. Let's surprise them with this. Would that be okay? Almost like our Christmas gift to each other and to him?"

"I'd like that. A lot." I moved toward her as she held out her arms to me. "I'm sorry for your suffering."

"I'm sorry for causing yours." She hugged me tightly. "Forgive me."

"Already done." I moved back and my heart filled with warmth beyond belief. I didn't have to let go of my dream of being Jeremy's wife. It was back within reach, and nothing was going to stop me from reaching out and taking hold of it.

25

JEREMY

"Hey. You okay?" My sister sat across from me at the kitchen table, half-eaten cookies strewn across the table in front of us.

"No. I already told you that I don't want to talk about this," I barked and hated myself for being hostile with her. She was my best friend. I gripped my face and let out another frustrating growl. "Why would Momma do this to me?"

"Because she thinks that she's protecting you, Jeremy. That is the only reasonable answer." She reached across and tugged my hands down. "She's not a monster. She's a good mom. A little cray-cray at times, but still, a really good mom."

I nodded, feeling like shit for being so ugly to her. "I know, but what the fuck?" I stood up and paced the floor. "Why would she attack Bailey like that?"

"You don't know what was said."

I whipped around and slammed my hands on the table. "Don't you dare take up for her right now."

My sister leaned back in her chair. "Don't yell at me. We're going to fix this. Just because Mom fucked things up does not mean the last word has been spoken. Give Bailey a day to chill out and call her. Go over there. Talk to her."

"I'm going tonight after I get Austin in bed." I walked over to the window as Nina's phone rang.

"Hello? Yeah, we're still over here at Jeremy's, Mom."

I turned around and crossed my arms over my chest as my sister glanced up at me.

"Okay. I'm glad you got to see her. Yeah, sure. We'll head over there now. Love you too." She put the phone down and stood up. "She talked to Bailey and apologized. Everything is going to be fine. She's cooking Christmas dinner and wants us there. Now."

"I'm not going until I know that she fixed this shit with my girl-friend." I walked around Nina and tried to storm into the hallway.

She grabbed my arm and pulled me back. "You are going because your son and your sister deserve a fucking Christmas, which includes dinner at Mom's house. Get your boots and your jacket and meet us in the car. She said she fixed it. She fixed it."

I wanted to bark at her again, but she was right. And I was being a dick. Big time.

"Fine. I'll be there in a second." I pulled out of her hold carefully and walked to my room. After closing the door, I got dressed and checked my phone. Nothing from Bailey. If mother had fixed every-thing, why the hell wasn't my girl calling me? I'd done nothing wrong. I was moving on with my life, letting go of my grief and taking steps forward *for* her. Just because my mother was batshit crazy didn't mean that I was.

I finished getting myself together and grabbed a baseball cap on the way out. There was no way I was fixing my hair or doing anything that my mother expected me to do. It was a proverbial finger in the air, and we would both know it.

"Hi, Daddy! You feeling better?" Austin leaned forward from the backseat and gripped my arm.

"Yeah, buddy. Sorry about that. Just a little misunderstanding with Granny. We're all good now." I buckled up and checked my phone as it dinged. I prayed like hell it was Bailey. Nope. Mayhem. "Hey. I need to run by the station before we head to Mom's."

My sister gave me a look. "Why?"

"The guys have something for me. It won't take more than a few seconds, I promise."

"You're not fighting another fire today, right, Dad?" Austin smiled as I turned to look at him in the backseat.

"Nope. I hope not." I winked and turned to my sister, who was in the driver's seat. "Ten minutes top."

"Alright. Sure." She pulled out of the driveway and drove toward the station.

I let my thoughts slip back to my date with Bailey a few weeks back. It was my favorite date thus far. We'd opened up in our conversation and talked about some of the deeper things in our lives, joked around the art gallery while all the stiffs in suits gave us dirty looks. We made fun of the stiffs, and ice skated until our thighs hurt. I made love to her all night long and held her tucked against me until the sun came up that next morning.

It was the kind of life I wanted to live every day, and it was so fucking close to being mine.

"I'm so scared I'm going to lose her." I kept my voice low and watched the snow drift by the car.

"You're not. I promise. I'll do anything I can to help make sure that doesn't happen." My sister squeezed my arm. "She loves you, Jeremy. It's going to take more than Mom acting up to push her away. Laila didn't run when Mom got nutty with her."

"Yeah, but Mom wasn't nearly as bad as she is now." I unbuckled as we got to the station. "I'll be right back guys."

"Hurry! I'm hungry," Austin said.

"You bet, buddy. Five minutes tops." I shut the door and jogged to the station. If was fucking freezing outside, and the snow seemed to be falling in blankets instead of cute little flakes. I walked in to hear the guys all laughing in the kitchen area. I walked that way and couldn't help but smile as they all called out to me. It was a warm welcome.

"Captain. You lazy mother fucker." Mayhem walked over and pulled me into a quick hug. "We've been missing you, man. What's up?"

"Just trying to give the little guy a Christmas." I shrugged and went around to shake everyone's hand.

"Well, we won't keep you here with us." He handed me a present in the shape of a clothing box.

"What's this?" I glanced down at it.

"A present?" Mayhem asked with his eyebrow raised, like we were all dumbasses, me especially.

"Fuck you too." I smiled and tore into it. I almost had the box opened when he stopped me.

"Wait. Chuck, tell Jeremy why we got him this just in case he forgot." Mayhem lifted his hands and laughed.

"Dude. You remember that crazy chick with black hair that your mother set you up with right after Laila died? The one we *never* thought we were going to get rid of?" Chuck smiled, and all the guys started to laugh loudly.

"The one that called me Captain Hotness all the time?" I lifted my eyebrow.

"That's the one!" Mayhem laughed and shook his head. "She brought brownies in here yesterday, for you of course, and we ate every damn one of them."

"And all of us got the shits." Chuck held his stomach as he laughed until his face turned red.

I laughed along with them. "Oh hell. She tried to give me the shits?"

"Open the box man, but yeah... that bitch tried to give you some EXLAX brownies, and we thought we were being smooth by eating your treats." He shook his head. "That's what we get, I guess."

"Idiots." I pulled out a bright orange hoodie and lifted it up. Captain Hotness was stitched across the front of it in big black lettering. "Brother."

The guys cracked up again, and I was rather glad they'd gotten the shits from eating my brownies. The asshats deserved it.

"Alright. I gotta get over to my mother's. Very funny." I tossed the box and the sweater in my office and jogged back out to the car. I got in and reached for the heater. "They're stupid. That was a waste of time."

"They just wanted to see you." Nina smiled and pulled out onto the street. "What did they get you?"

I explained in a PG way, and she and Austin both had a good laugh on the way over to my mom's house. By the time we got there, I felt much better. I wasn't ready to get out of the car and attack anyone. I was looking for ways to make things right. I'd apologize to my mother and hear her out, have dinner with the family and then go looking for Bailey. I wanted resolution. Now.

"I love Granny's pineapples and ham!" Austin yelled from the backseat and bounded out into the snow, leaving his door open.

"Hey. Your door," I called after him, but he kept running for the house.

My mom opened the door and picked him up, swinging him around as Nina, and I got the rest of the presents out of the trunk, closed up the car and walked into the scent of Christmas Day.

I breathed in deeply and turned as my mom reached out and grabbed my arms. "I'm so sorry, Jeremy. I was trying to protect you, but you don't need me to do that anymore. I just can't get past the fact that you're going to be okay without me, and that you will heal from Laila."

I nodded. "I'm sorry too." I pulled her close and bit my tongue. I wanted to ask if she *really* went to see Bailey, but as soon as I turned the corner, the question was null and void.

Bailey was wrapped up in my mom's favorite blanket with Austin on her lap and a Christmas storybook in her lap. He was bouncing around, and she was laughing as she kissed the side of his face.

"Thank God," I whispered as I moved into the room and knelt beside her. "You scared me so bad." I leaned down, cupped her face and kissed her several times as Austin moved off her lap.

"Come on, Austin. Let's put whipped cream on our hot chocolate. Granny needs your help." My mom and Nina left the living room, and I stood, half-dragging Bailey with me.

"Jeremy. I just-"

"Hush." I leaned down and kissed her again as I wrapped my arms around her and pinned her to my chest. I made sweet love to her mouth as I memorized the softness of her lips and drank in the taste of chocolate and cherries on her tongue. By the time we pulled back, we were both breathless, our cheeks pink.

"Wow." I kissed her again and pressed my forehead to hers. "I don't know what happened with my mom last night-"

"It doesn't matter. We worked it out." She moved back and ran her hands up my chest to cup my neck. "I'm sorry I left a note."

"No, baby. I'm sorry she upset you. When I got up this morning, and you weren't there," I paused to take a shaky breath, "I thought maybe I'd lost you. I don't want to feel that way ever again until we're old and have had our fucking fortieth wedding anniversary. You hear me?"

She tilted her head and lifted an eyebrow. "Fortieth anniversary?"

"Long story, but I want this thing between us. I want you to have my babies, Bailey. I want your shit all over my house; your warm, sexy, little body pressed to mine at night." I pulled her in for another long kiss as I ran my hands over her back to her ass and squeezed tightly. "Don't leave me again. I don't want to live my life worried that I'm being set up for another loss. I can't handle that."

"I want that too. So badly." She wrapped herself around me and let out a soft sigh. "I'd never leave you, Jeremy. Not ever. You're all I've ever wanted in my life."

I moved back and forced her to look up at me. "Good, because you're stuck. I love you like a fat kid loves chocolate cake."

"I love you like a stripper loves a pole."

"I love you like-" I started, but my sister cut me off.

"Oh God. Get off it already. The hot chocolate is cooling." She shook her head and walked back to the kitchen, mumbling under her breath, 'like whipped cream love a cuppa hot chocolate.'

"Oh!" I laughed and pulled Bailey into my arms again. "I'm going to ask you to be my wife pretty soon. Did you know that? I don't wanna wait."

"And I'm going to say yes. I don't want another day without you."

"Such a good girl." I leaned down and nipped at her lips.

"All yours, Captain Hotness." She laughed as I chased her into the kitchen.

"Wait. Where did you hear about that crazy lune from?" I glanced between Nina, my mom, and Bailey. How the fuck did Bailey know the Captain Hotness story?

"Wasn't me." My mom shrugged and turned.

"No clue." My sister smiled and went back to working on drinks.

"Who wants some hot chocolate?" Bailey asked, and everyone busted out laughing - but me.

"Austin? Save me from too many women in my life." I walked back into the living room looking for the little man.

"Nope. Not me, Daddy. I'm thinking I'm going to wait until I see evidence and then I'll help."

"Evidence of what?" I knelt beside him with confusion on my face.

"Of girls sloughing off their cooties skin. Until then? You're on your own."

I laughed until my sides hurt. Life couldn't be better, and though I'd lost so much over the short number of years that I drew air into my lungs, I had gained so much too.

Nothing would ever be the same, but it would be just as good.

Just as good, in a different way.

EPILOGUE

BAILEY

Six Months Later

"I'm scared!" I moved into Jeremy's arms as we stood in the center of the art museum. "What if they hate it?"

"Then they're idiots." He leaned down and kissed me a few times. "You're brilliant, Bailey. They're going to love it."

I turned in his arms and glanced up as they unveiled my first painting. Everyone clapped and cheered around us, and I let out a long sigh of relief. Whether they really liked it or not, the moment was over, and we hadn't heard complete silence.

"Thank God." I turned to face him. "Why was that so hard?"

"Because it meant something to you." He touched the side of my face. "I'm so proud of you baby. Going after something you've wanted to do your whole life."

"Are we talking about you or the painting?" I offered him a cheeky grin.

"You've wanted to *do* me your whole life? Slut." He chuckled as I popped him in the chest. "Oh, Nina and Mom are here with Austin. Let's go catch up with them."

"Does this dress look okay? It's obvious that I'm five months pregnant and *not* just chunky, right?"

He wrapped his arm around my shoulders. "Please do not make me take you back into a storeroom and fuck you silly in your pretty dress to remind you how fucking hot you look. Cause I will."

I smiled. "Please?"

"Ugh. I married a good girl, and she quickly turned into a bad girl." He moved his arm from my shoulders to the back of my waist with his hand resting on the top curve of my ass. My hormones were all over the place thanks to the pregnancy. We'd fucked three times before coming to the event, and I'd sucked him off in the car on the way over. It was getting a little ridiculous. He was fighting the good fight, but I could tell he was exhausted.

"How is my grandbaby?" Jeremy's mom moved up to me and put her hands on my swollen stomach.

"Good. We're all good, Mom." Jeremy bent down and picked up Austin. "And me and this guy are hoping for another boy. We gotta even this thing out!"

"I wouldn't mind a sister," Austin offered and smiled over at me.

"Hey! We made a deal. I give you twenty dollars, and you help me talk about the baby being a boy, so we make sure if God is listening that he actually hears us." Jeremy gave Austin a look.

We all laughed together.

"Come with me and let's check out the children's room, Aus." Nina reached out for Austin and took him off to another room as Jeremy's mother turned to us and let out a contented sigh.

"I'm so proud of you both." She reached out and gripped my hand as she looked back and forth between us. "You've had a lot of curve balls, but you've pulled together and done a great job of figuring things out."

"Well, like I've said before," Jeremy started, "I knew I was going to propose in the spring, I just didn't expect to get married in the same few weeks, but it's been good. No need to drag anything out."

"Especially with a baby coming." I rubbed my belly and glanced down, still a little overwhelmed that we were pregnant.

"Enjoy your night. I'm going to go mingle with the upper class and work to make them feel small." She smirked and walked off as Jeremy, and I chuckled.

"You look good." I turned toward him and pressed my hands to his chest. "Really good."

"You horny again? Already?" He paled a little, which caused me to laugh.

I nodded. "Really bad. My pussy hurts."

"Because I've fucked it ten times today." He pulled me close and kissed me a few times. "Storeroom?"

"Mmmmm... storeroom please." I held his hand as we walked through the crowds of people that tried to stop us. My sexy husband opened every door and poked his head in until he found the right place. He pulled me inside and closed the door behind us. We were plunged into darkness until he reached up and pulled the string dangling above our heads.

I laughed nervously.

"Turn around, baby girl. Let's take care of you." He spun me around and tugged my dress up over my ass. "No panties? You dirty little slut."

"God yes." I lifted my foot and rested it on a footstool in front of me. "Fuck me hard, okay?"

"No one would believe this shit if I even thought to tell them." The sound of his zipper had my heart racing. Most women had odd cravings for food, but mine was for his dick. I loved it so damn much, and I couldn't seem to get enough of it. It was almost embarrassing, but he wouldn't let it be.

"Don't tell anyone that. I'll end up on a sweater or something." I pressed my hands against the wall in front of me as he gripped my hips and drove his thick shaft into my wet slit.

We moaned together and moved in tandem, fucking each other with little grunts and moans until I was right at the edge.

"Fuck, Bailey. Tell me you're there, Angel. Your little pussy is contracting like a vise grip around me. I'm so close to unloading myself inside of you. Come with me."

"I'm there," I mumbled and cried out in ecstasy as he drove himself deeper inside of me. Electricity burst from the center of my stomach, and it was all I could do to hold onto the wall and take the power of his fucking.

He finally slowed and moved back. "You're going to be the death of me."

"No. Not a chance." I turned and pressed my back against the wall as I let out a sigh of relief. "Thank you. I'm good for at least a few hours."

"A few hours?" His voice rose to a high pitch.

"Should I get a vibrator?" I smiled and gripped the front of his button-down shirt. He looked so proper in his black tie get up.

"Fuck no. I got this under control." He gave me a scared look as he trapped me against the wall behind me. "You want the D? You get the D."

I smiled. "I want it again."

"Holy shit."

I laughed loudly. "No, I just want you. Kiss me like you mean it."

He leaned in and nipped at my lips before kissing me good and hard. "Oh, I mean it alright. You're mine, baby girl. Forever."

Crazy enough, forever didn't seem nearly long enough.

ABOUT THE AUTHOR

I'm a former firefighter/EMS guy who's picked up the proverbial pen and started writing bad boy romance stories. I co-write with my sister, Ali Parker as we travel the United States for the next two years.

You're going to find Billionaires, Bad Boys, Mafia and loads of sexiness. Something for everyone, hopefully. I'd love to connect with you.

www.westonparkerbooks.com

Made in the USA
Columbia, SC
24 November 2020